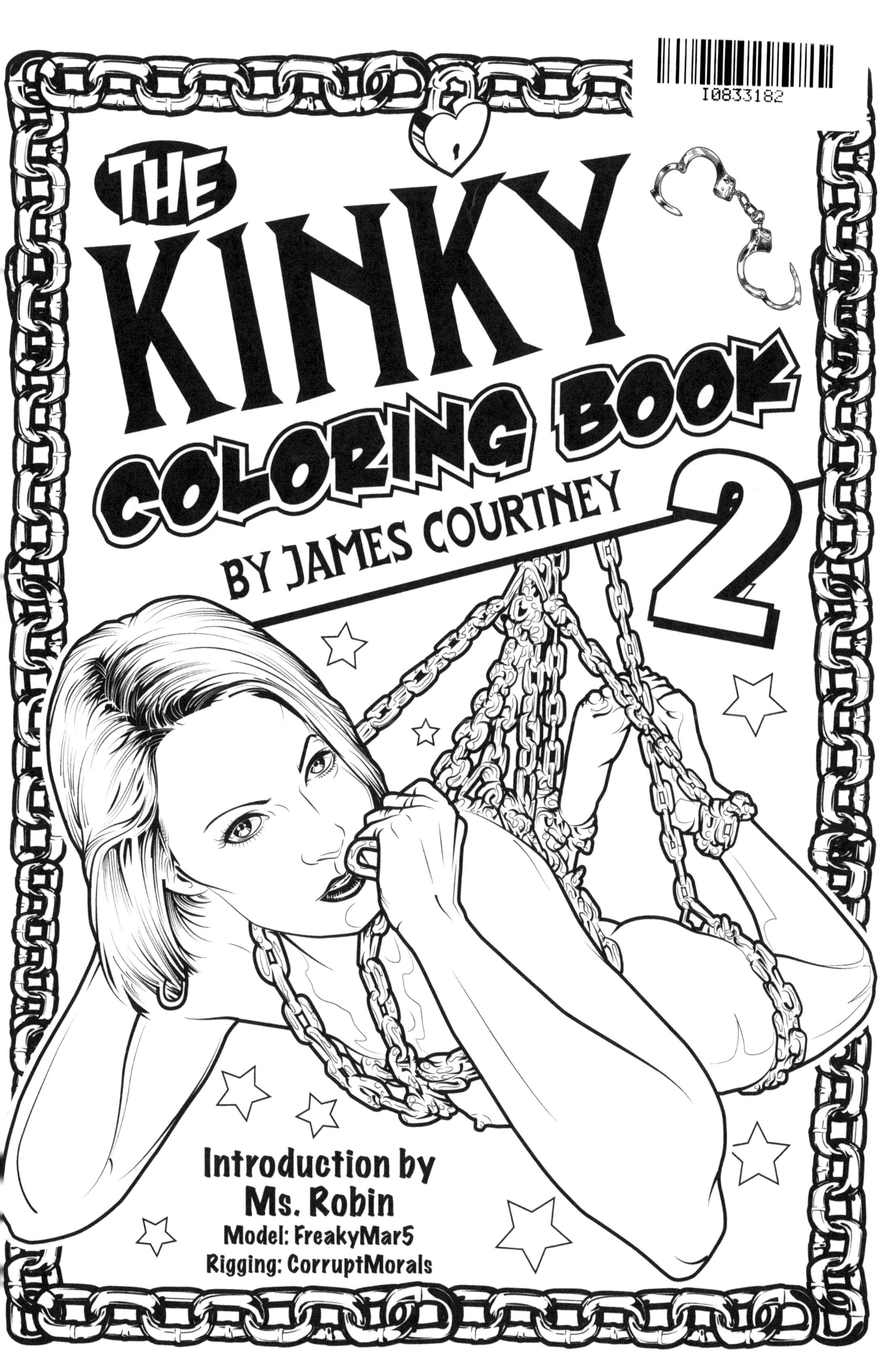
THE
KINKY
COLORING BOOK
2
BY JAMES COURTNEY
Introduction by
Ms. Robin
Model: FreakyMar5
Rigging: CorruptMorals
I0833182

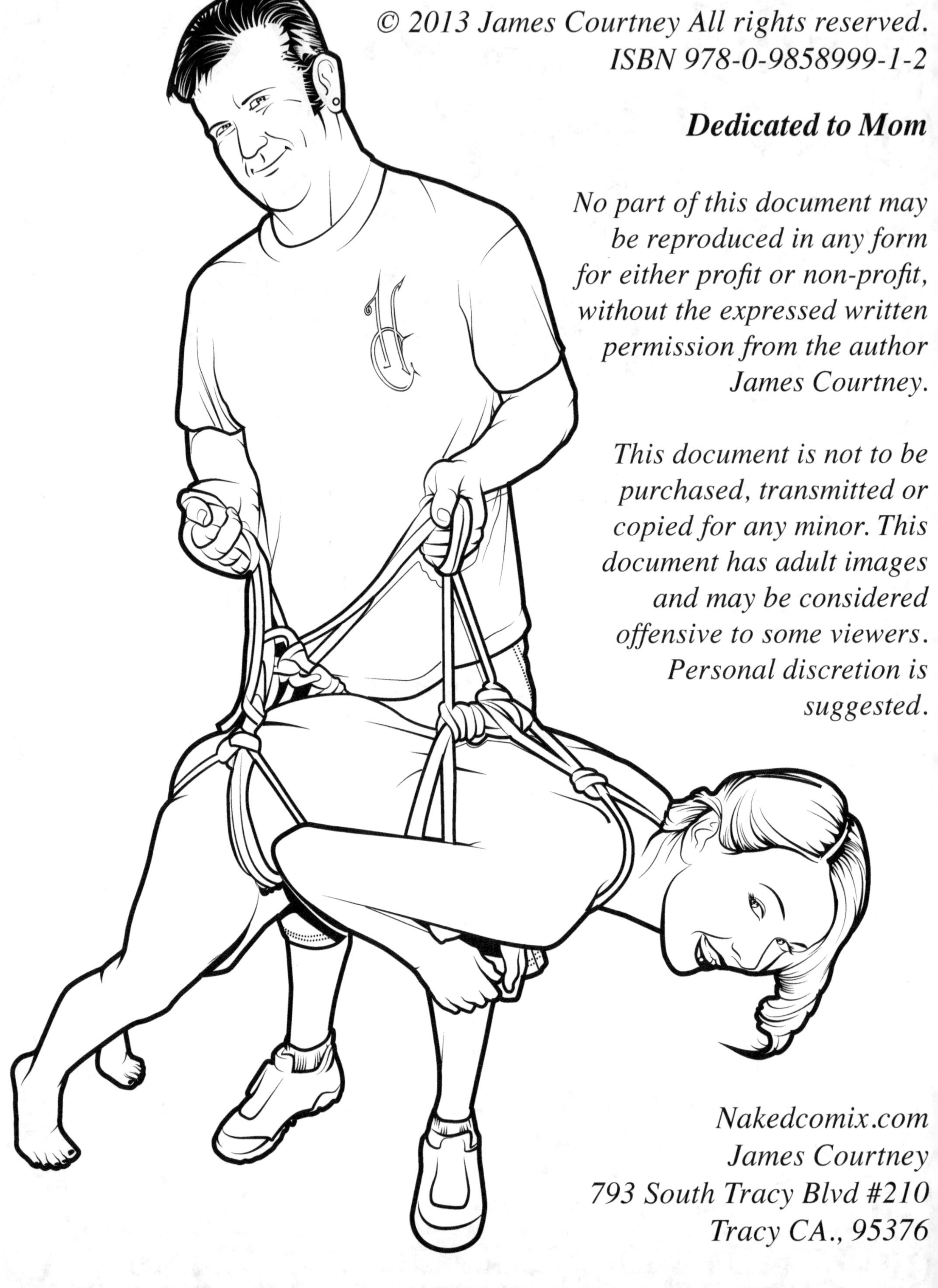

The Kinky Coloring Book 2
By James Courtney

ISBN 978-0-9858999-1-2

Dedicated to Mom

Nakedcomix.com
James Courtney
793 South Tracy Blvd #210
Tracy CA., 95376

I first discovered Nakedcomix through a close friend, CorruptMorals, who is a rope rigger, welder, carpenter, model, and all-around maker-of-mischief. CorruptMorals told me one day "Some artist wants me to tie a girl to a motorcycle for a photo shoot." My first thought was, ooh, that's sexy and intriguing. As he told me more about Nakedcomix and James Courtney as an illustrator, my piqued interest turned into fascination.

Perusing the Nakedcomix website, I was drawn in by the bold colors, mischievous situations, and enticing range of strong, beautiful women. Something unexpected kept pulling me back. With most erotic images, I see them, feel aroused, and move on – there's no deeper connection. But the world I discovered in Nakedcomix mixed comic book themes with beautiful half-clothed women, and a relentlessly joyful sense of humor. Each illustration was unique, flirtatious, inviting - but it was also something more. In the confidence of each woman's body, and behind their engaging eyes, I could see a different story. Fully formed, welcoming characters, each of them was thoroughly enjoying themselves. They always left me wanting more.

I asked James if I could interview him about his art for an article I wanted to write about him. Thus began the first of many intense and creative discussions about what makes good erotic art. James and I quickly became friends—after all, we shared a love of great art and beautiful women. Over coffee, to the sometime dismay (and sometime arousal) of random coffee shop eavesdroppers, we talked about what defines the Nakedcomix aesthetic. Courtney's art rejects the trend of the "distant beauty" in erotic art, and puts the viewer in immediate relationship with the subject. The playful tease of a Gil Elvgren pinup meets the bold lines of a classic comic book, with a contemporary twist that showcases each model's individual personality.

I find each of James' illustrations to be a down-to-earth (or, sometimes, out-of-this-world) celebration of each individual's sexiness. I can relate to each of them, and have fun imagining what will happen to them next. Their attractiveness doesn't lie solely in the attributes of their bodies. I see it in the mixture of surprise and arousal when literal electricity courses through the scene. I see it in the beaming, adoring face of a slave looking at her master. As James has expanded the material in this second Kinky Coloring Book to include more men, different body types, and even more diverse sexy situations—I find that underlying message has become stronger. We are all sexy! It is the magical ability of James, his camera, and his illustrations to capture each moment of erotic fire and delight in his models' eyes, and share it with you in the pages that follow.

James shared his excitement about an erotic art project where any viewer could discover and exercise their creativity, by coloring the image in their own way. In July of 2012, James published his first Kinky Coloring Book. We giggled over the sexy science experiments, fantasy creatures, and noir femme fatales that made up that book, and I sent copies to some very lucky friends. We talked in-depth about his process—setting up photo shoots to create visual references, and turning those photographs into imaginative illustrations. I shared my excitement about that indefinable something more that I find in Nakedcomix art. We both agreed—through round after round of discussion—that erotic art like Nakedcomix can also be viewed as feminist art. Since a primary goal of feminism is to interrogate and overcome objectification, any erotic art that engages the model as an individual, not an object, is feminist art. James takes the time to think about the inner beauty that makes each model sexy – and what kind of personal relationship he can develop between model and viewer.

Prepare yourself for a journey through a wild landscape—you'll meet vicious sea creatures, mad scientists, damsels in distress, fierce clowns, and wind up toys. —and all of them entirely erotic. They invite you in, to play with them and bring them to life with your own colors. So have some fun and make some sexy art with us.

Ms. Robin is a writer, artist, masochist, and all-around kinkster. Her erotica has been published on the Good Vibes Blog, and you can follow her NSFW tweets @robinerotica.

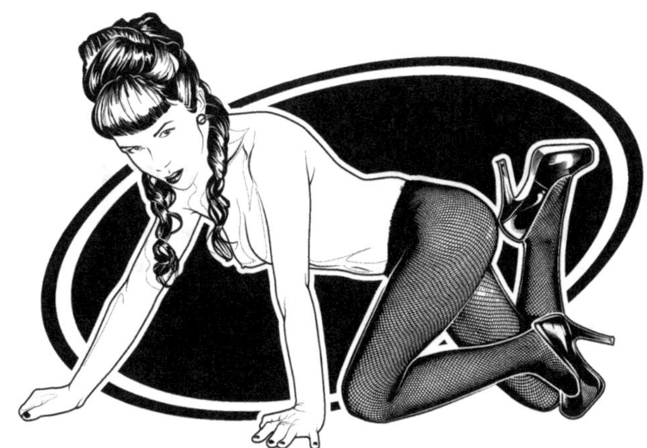

To the right, Model: Libby Loo
Opposite page, Models: CorruptMorals & Raven Le Faye
Front Cover, Models: Raven Le Faye and Chelsea Christian

According to ScarletCamellia, this is the first time anyone has documented her angry face. That's a shame, since it looks kind of hot. But so do the branding irons and both can be dangerous to play with.

Branding

Models: ScarletCamellia & CorruptMorals

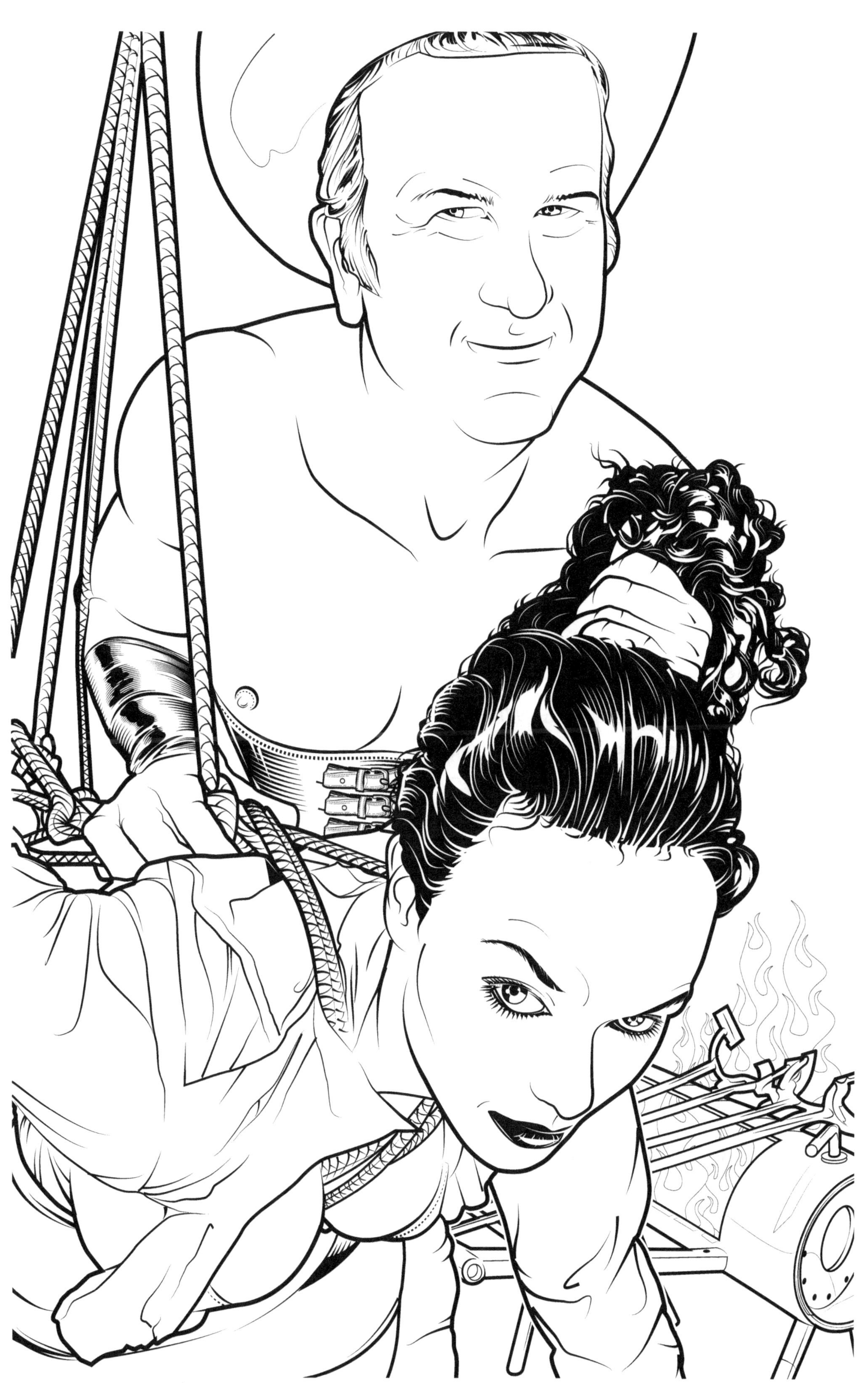

To be honest, a large part of me wants to see people's heads explode when they try to color in all this fine detail. I wonder if that makes me a coloring book sadist?

Cherry Blossom Geisha

Model: Cherry Katonic

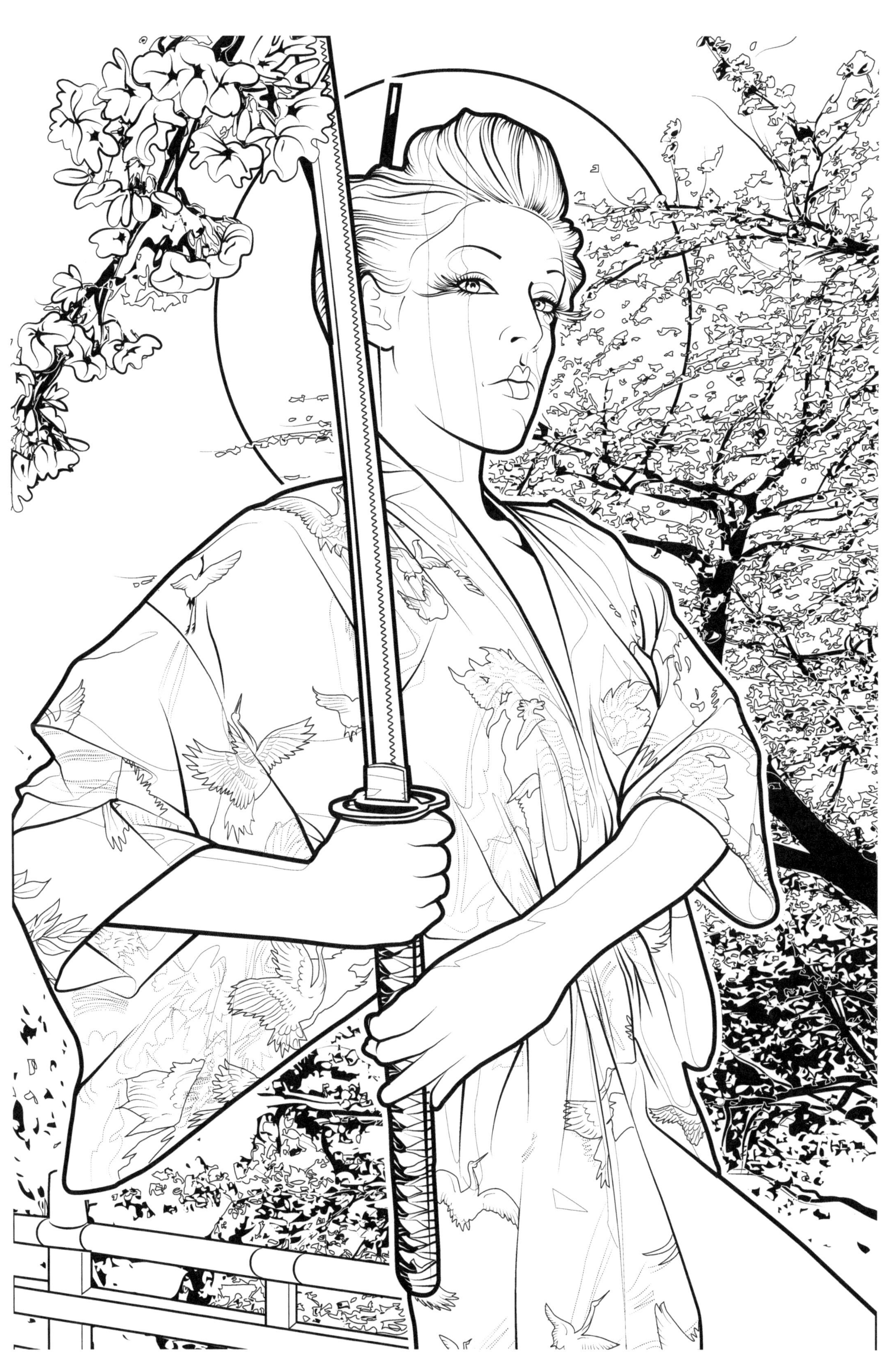

Tied up so pretty...
She waits for pleasure and pain...
Ready for it now?

Haiku by Ms Robin

Collared

Model: Raven Le Faye, Rigging: CorruptMorals

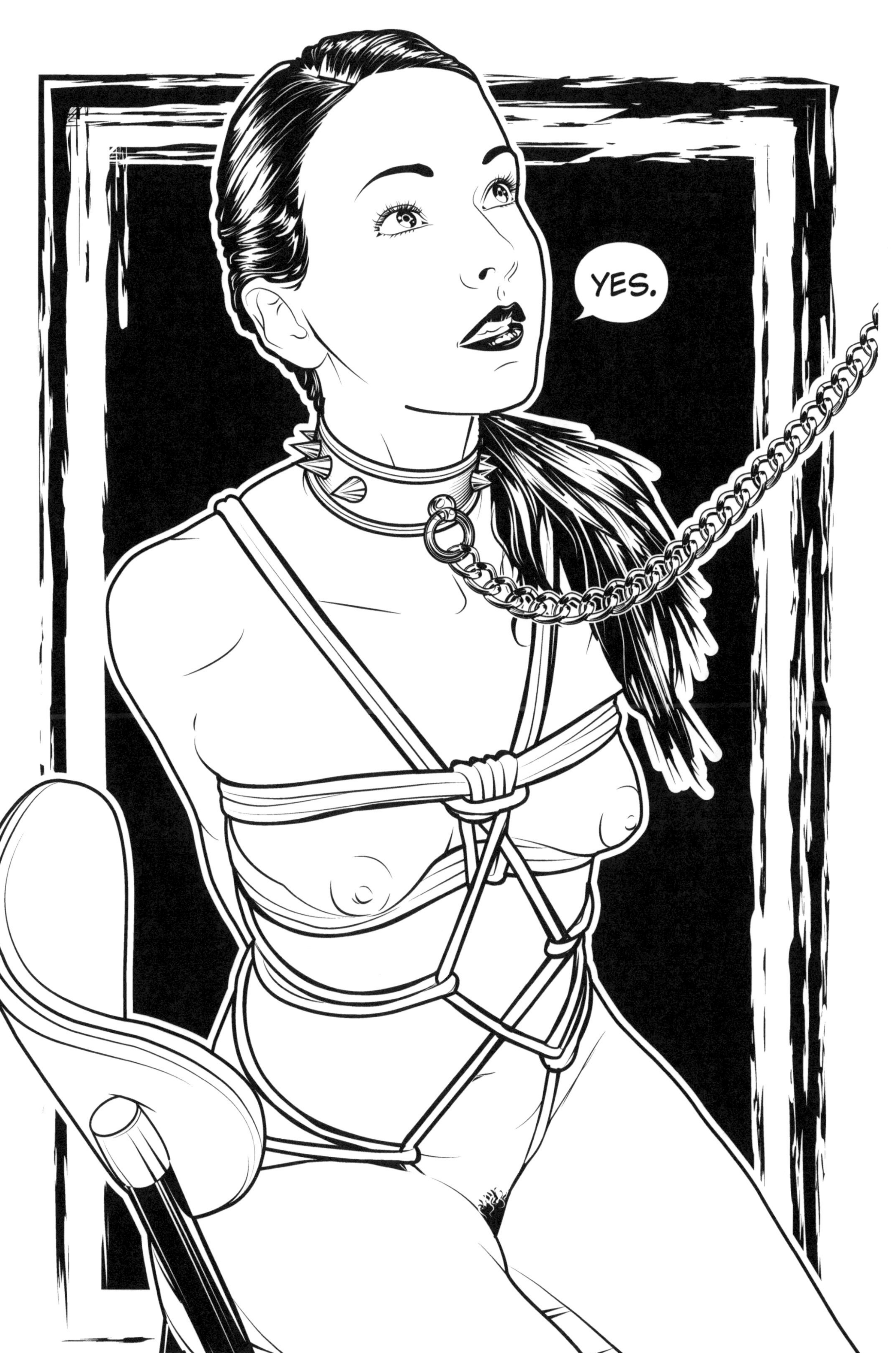
YES.

The Cold War may be over, but some of its heat still remains.

Comrade Kory

Model: Kory Vixen

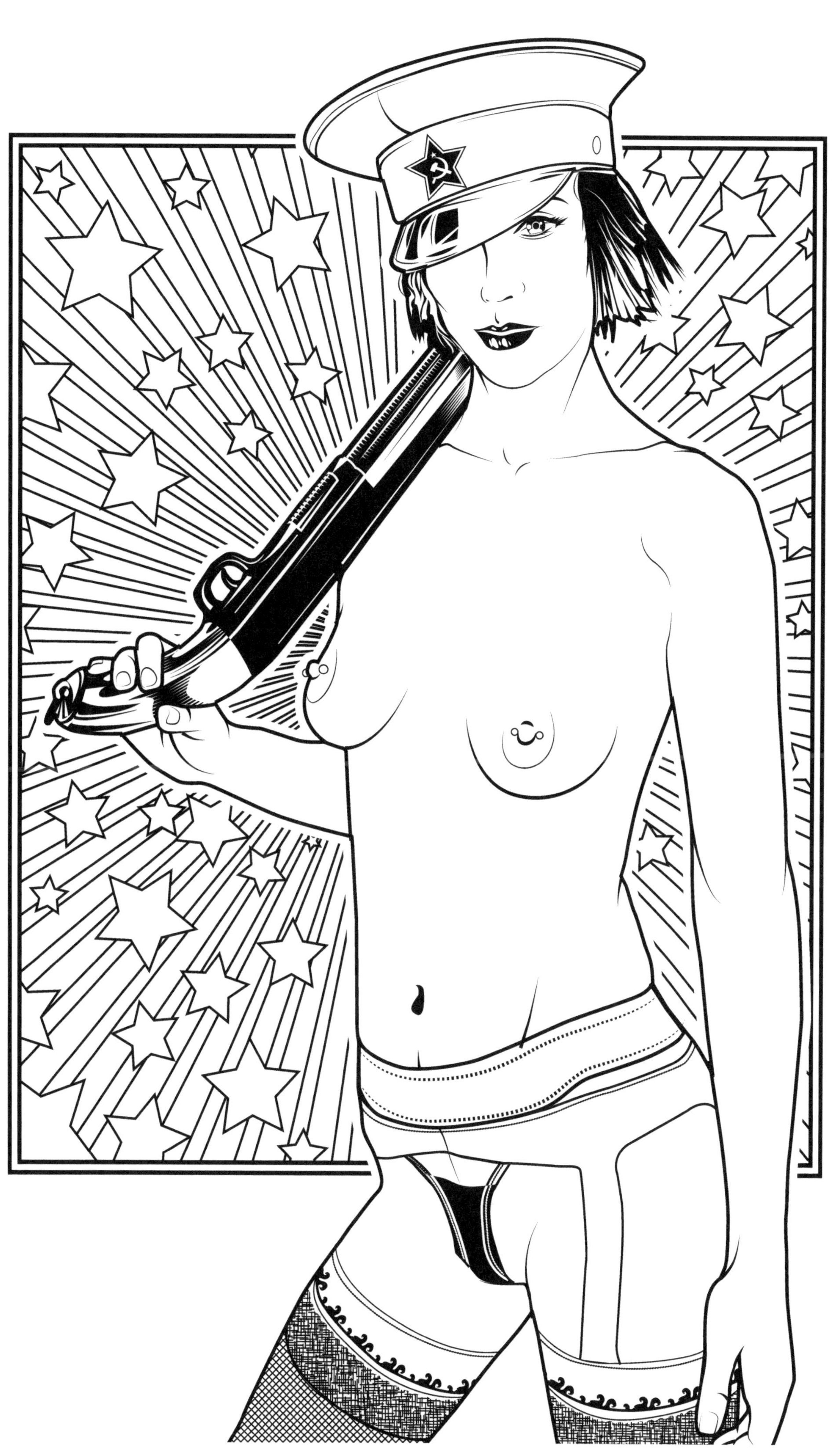

This started as a black and white illustration that I later used as a promotional poster for the band Puff Puff Beer. Here it is without the extra copy. The title of their CD was "Great Decisions". When I asked them what that meant, they said it referred to the type of "...great decisions you make at 2 in the morning after drinking all night."

Tattooing Courtney

Model: Courtney Cass

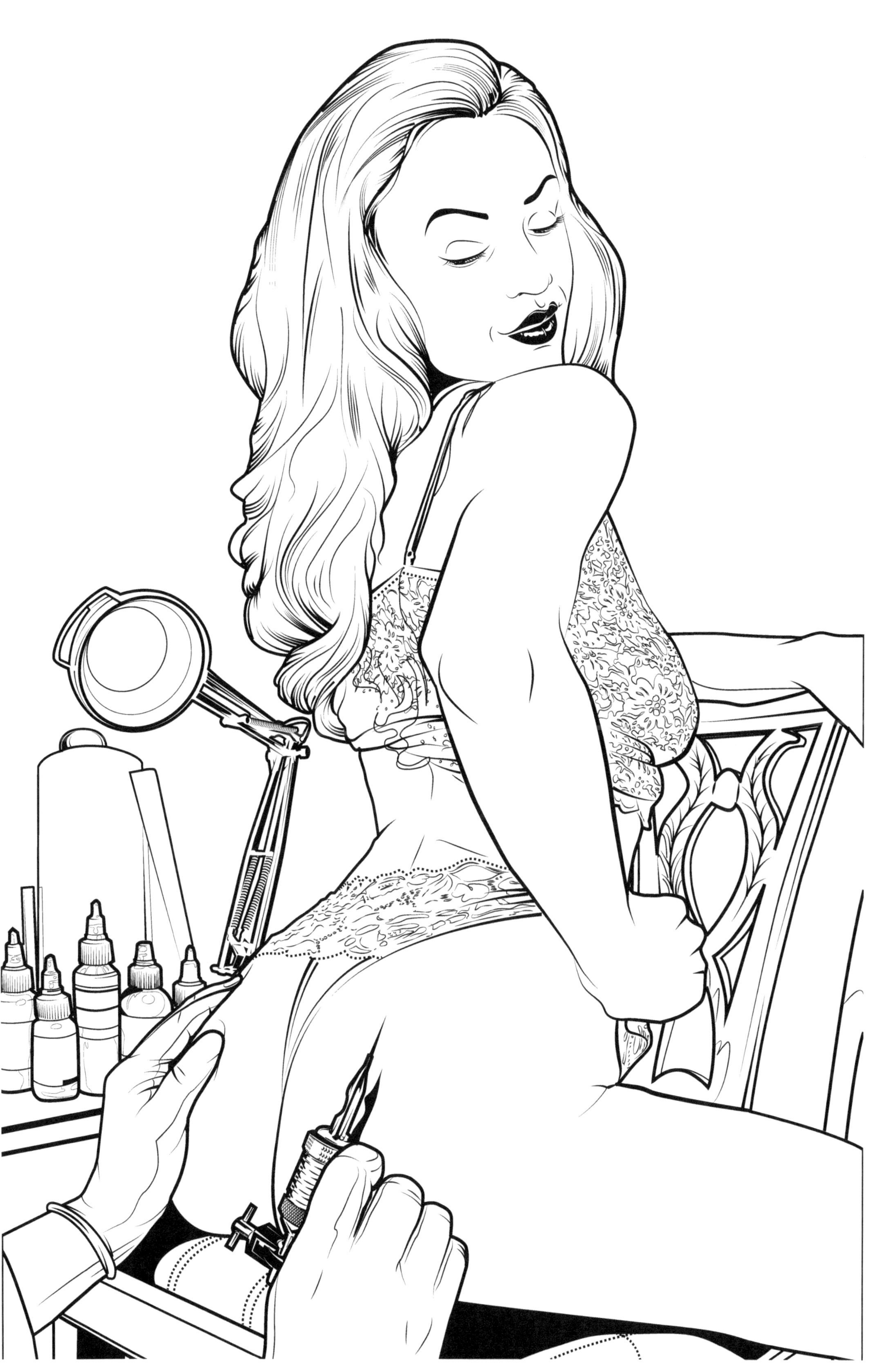

As a former derby girl, latex clothes designer and founder of Lust Designs, she is pretty accomplished for a "Bad" Penny!

We All Scream For Ice Cream

Model: Penny McClish

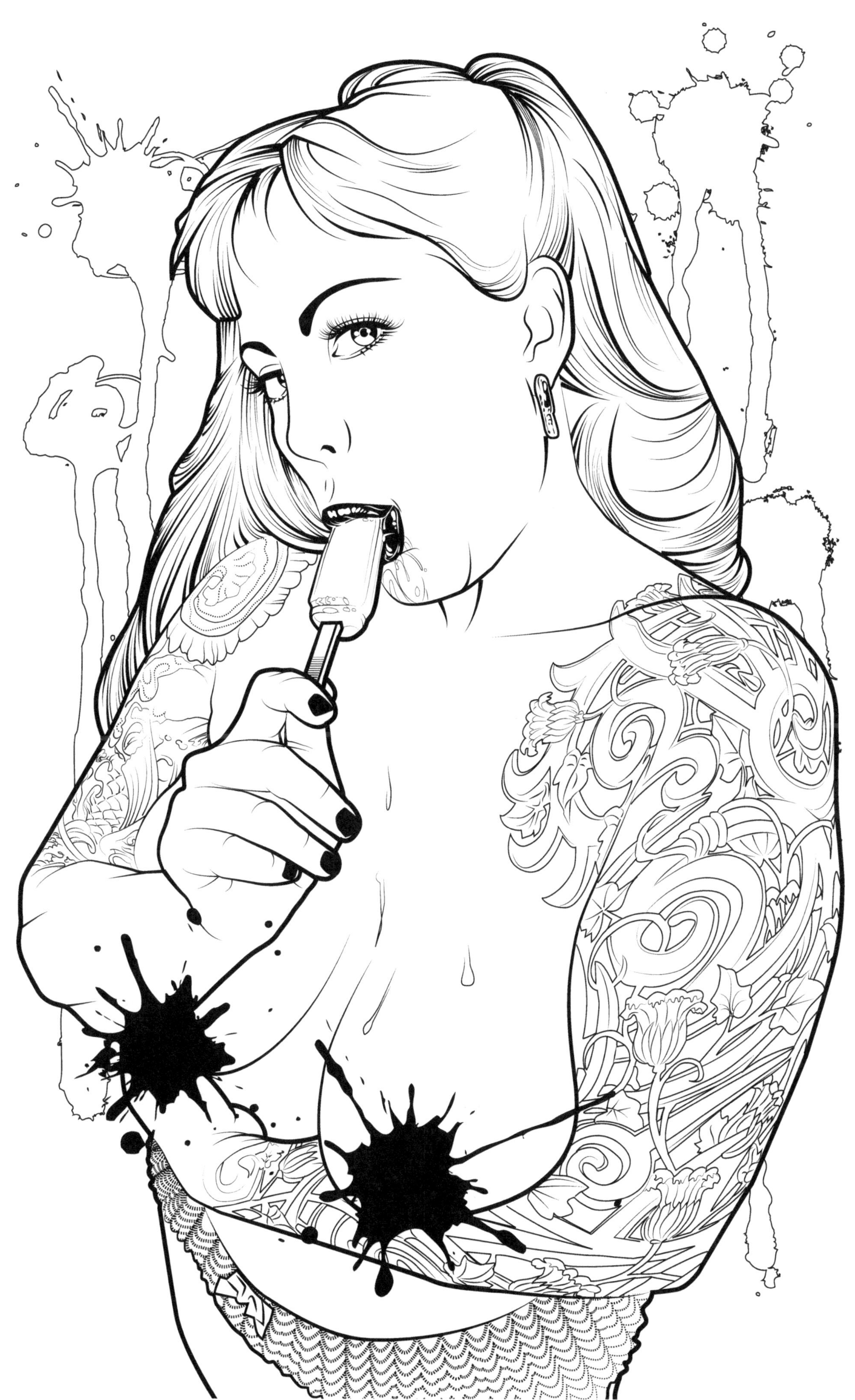

I have to admit to taking some artistic license here. Because anyone with a ounce of gun safety awareness knows you should never carry a firearm like this. It just looks so cool with the tutu and the wings, though.

Fairy Force Five

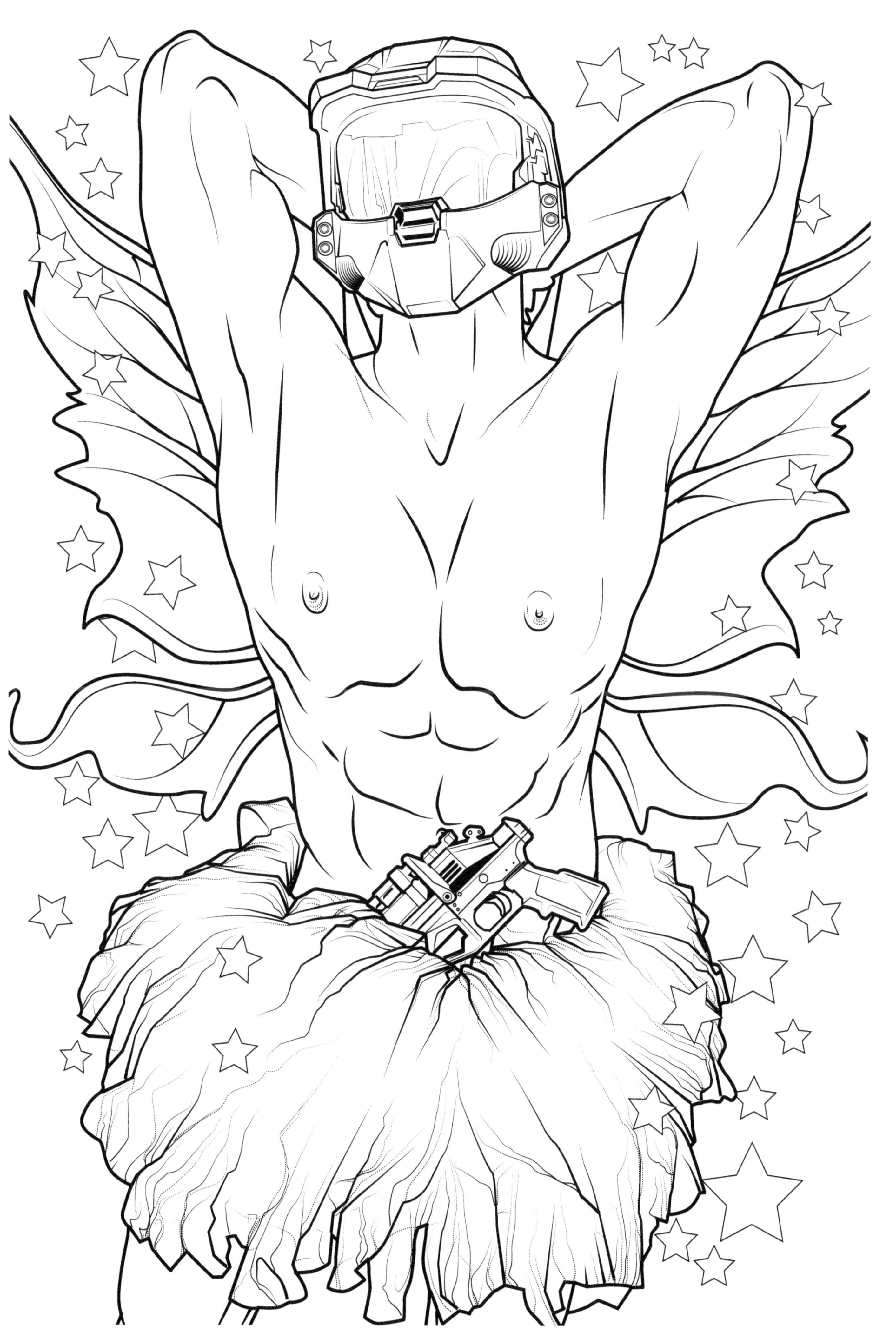

Dizzy is always going on about how much she likes working with Jeff. I believe the truth is she just likes sitting on him while holding sharp objects to his throat.

Pirate Queen

Models: Dizzy Night and Jeff Cathcart

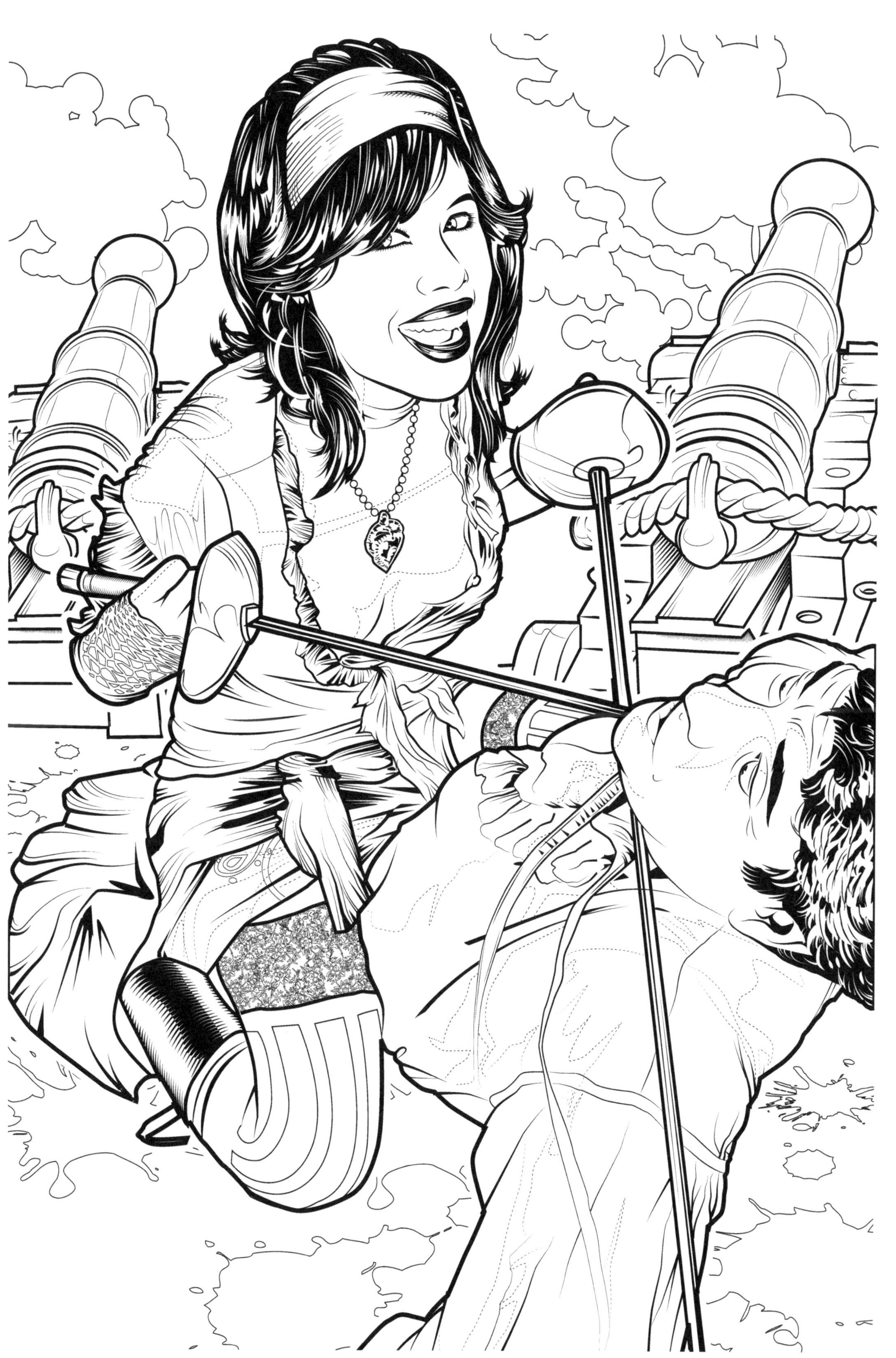

Amazingly enough, this was from Eleanor's first, ever rope bondage shoot. Some of the more fearless fetish models, it seems, just like to start out in the deep end of the pool.

The Hanging Woman

Model: Eleanor, Rigger: CorruptMorals

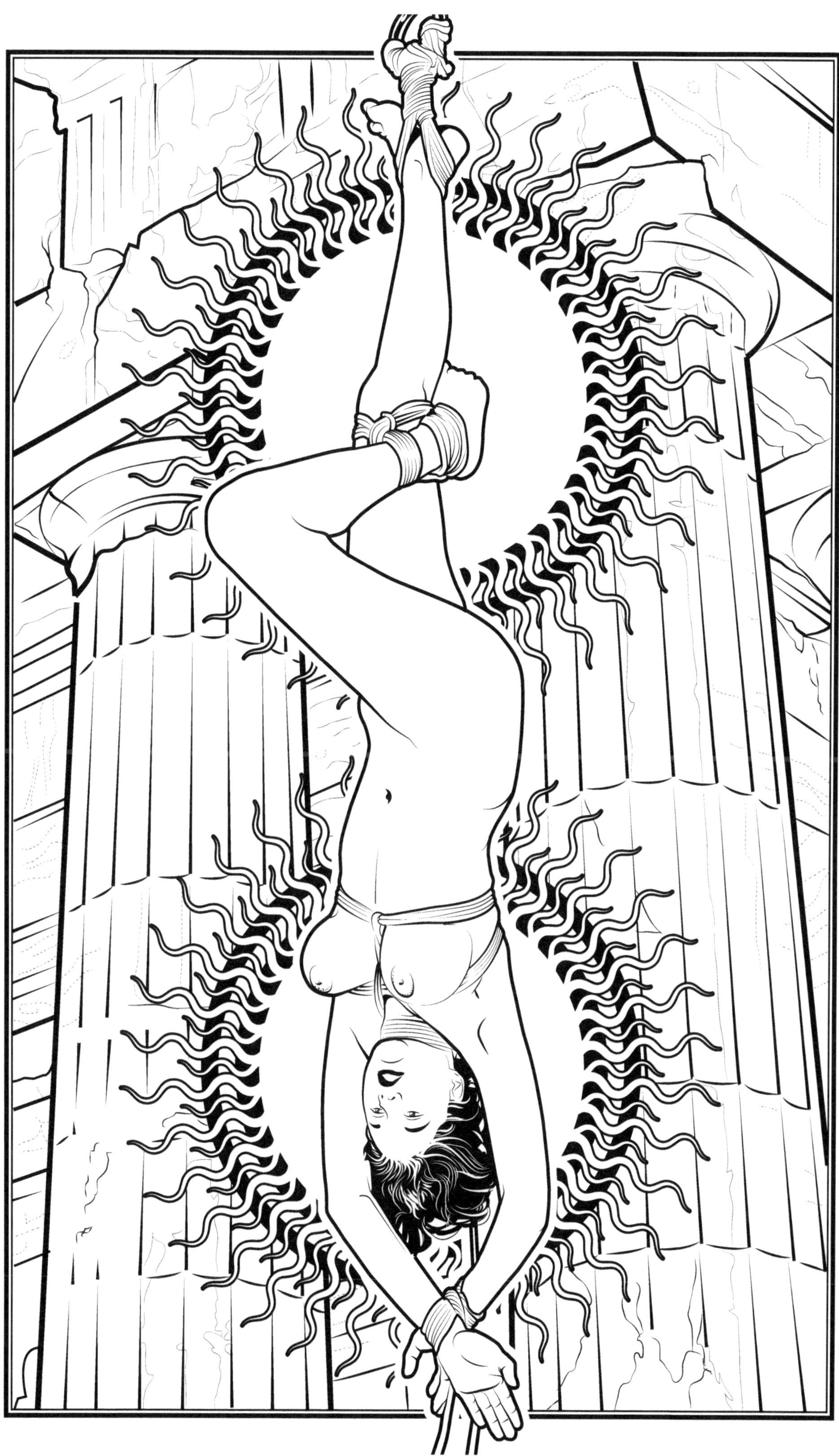

"The more a thing is perfect, the more it feels pleasure and pain."

Dante Alighieri, The Divine Comedy

Fallen

Model: Scarlet Faux

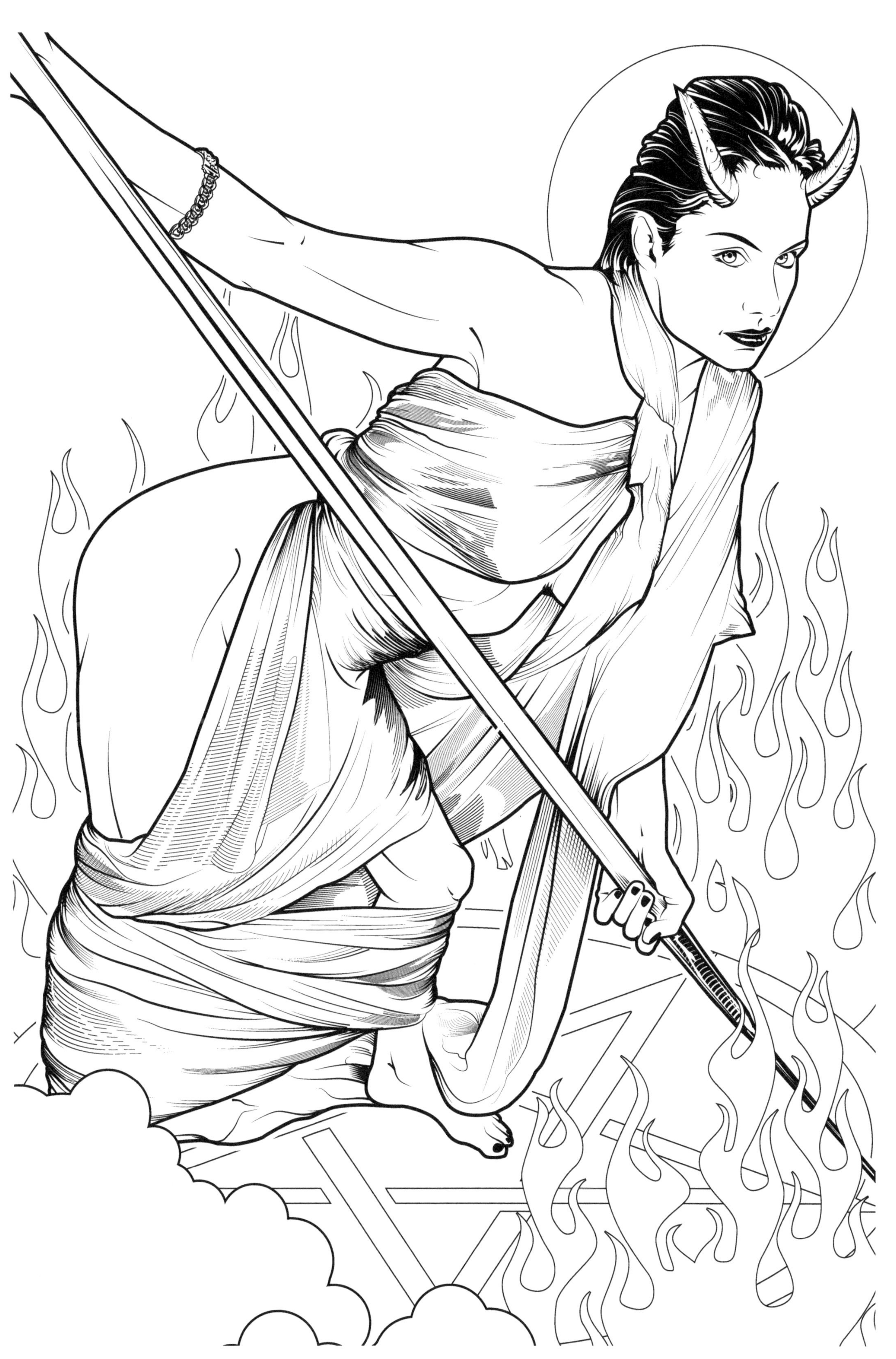

I think of this as sort of Art Nouveau meets Penthouse. I wonder if Alphonse Mucha were still alive, whether he'd be doing erotica? One would hope.

Worshiping The Goddess

Models: Daledoe & Roisbi2

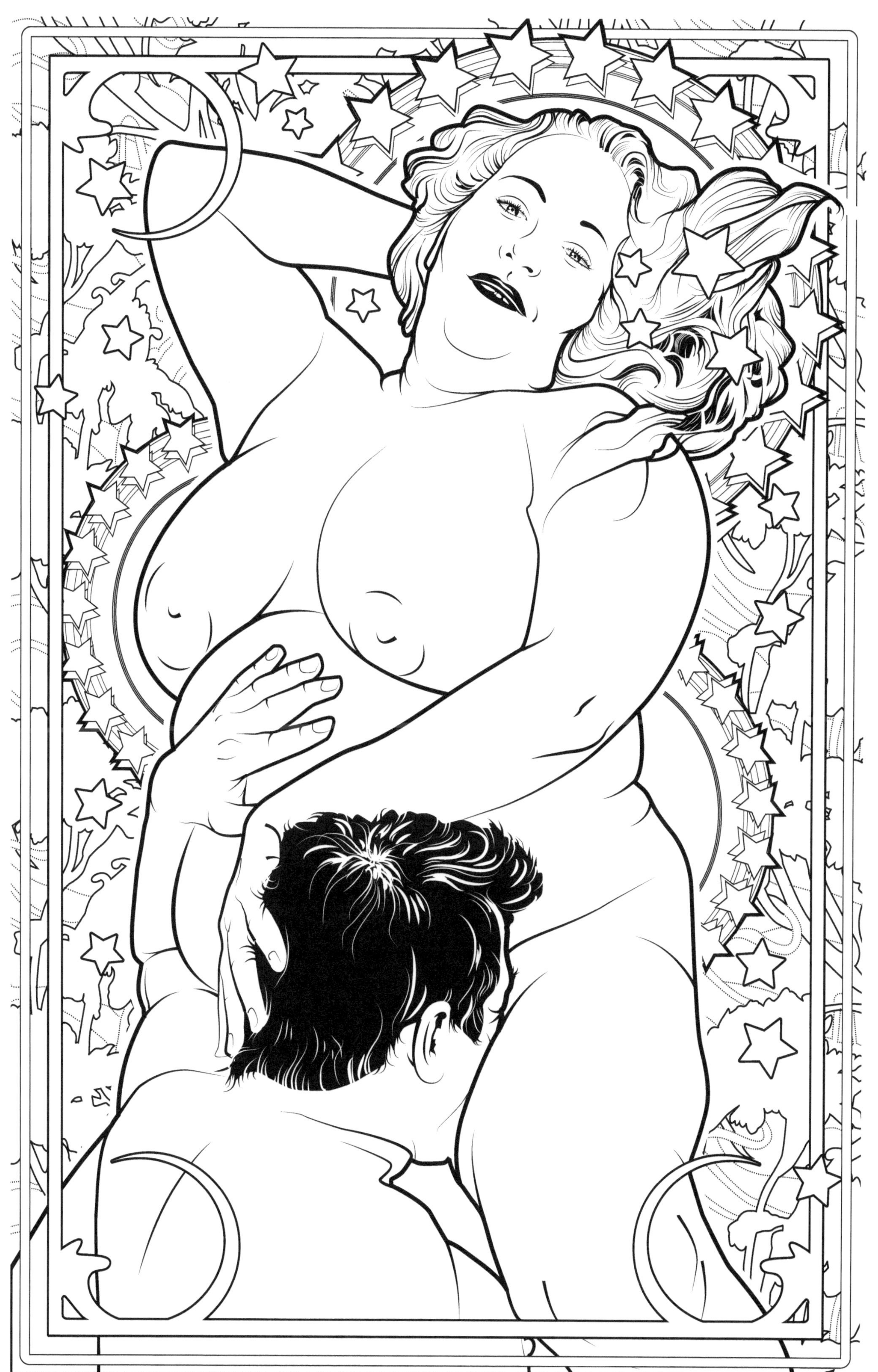

Some things should not be hurried.
Because, to be honest, a lot of the fun in life is in the journey, not just arriving at your destination.

Lay Over

Models: Honey Baby88 & Patrick

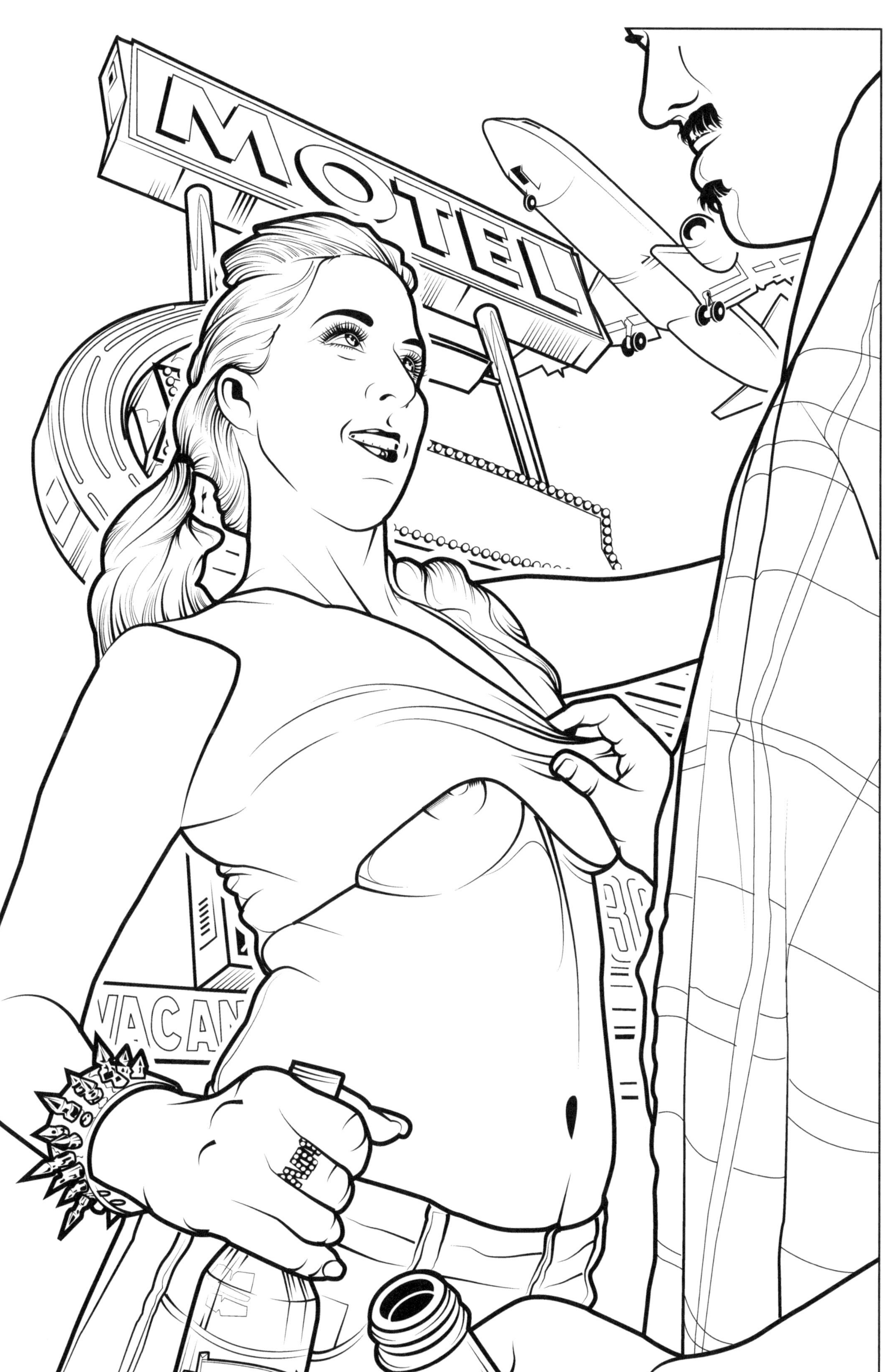
MOTEL
VACAN

The comic book geek in me had a lot of fun with the details in this Damsel In Distress picture. I even took the time to make up a press pass and newspaper for her. Of course, Scarlet Camilla wouldn't be waiting for some dork in red and blue underwear to rescue her.

No Rescue

Model: ScarletCamellia, Rigging: CorruptMorals

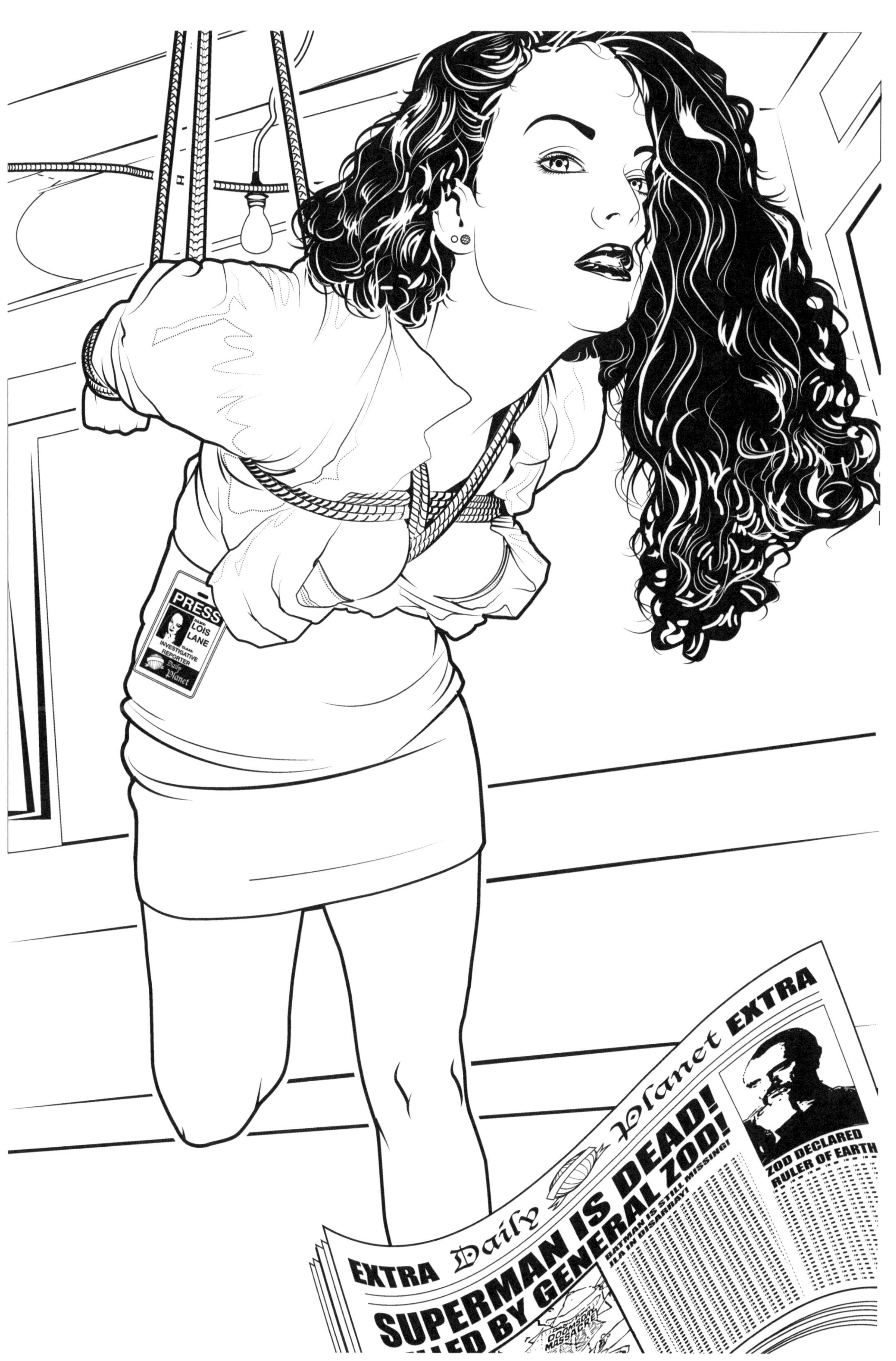
PRESS
NAME:
LOIS
LANE
CLASS:
INVESTIGATIVE
REPORTER
Daily Planet
EXTRA Daily Planet EXTRA
EXTRA
SUPERMAN IS DEAD!
BY GENERAL ZOD!
BATMAN IS STILL MISSING!
JLA IN DISARRAY!
ZOD DECLARED
RULER OF EARTH

The higher up you go, the better chance to see angels as they fall.

Over The City

Models: Eleanor and Raven Le Faye

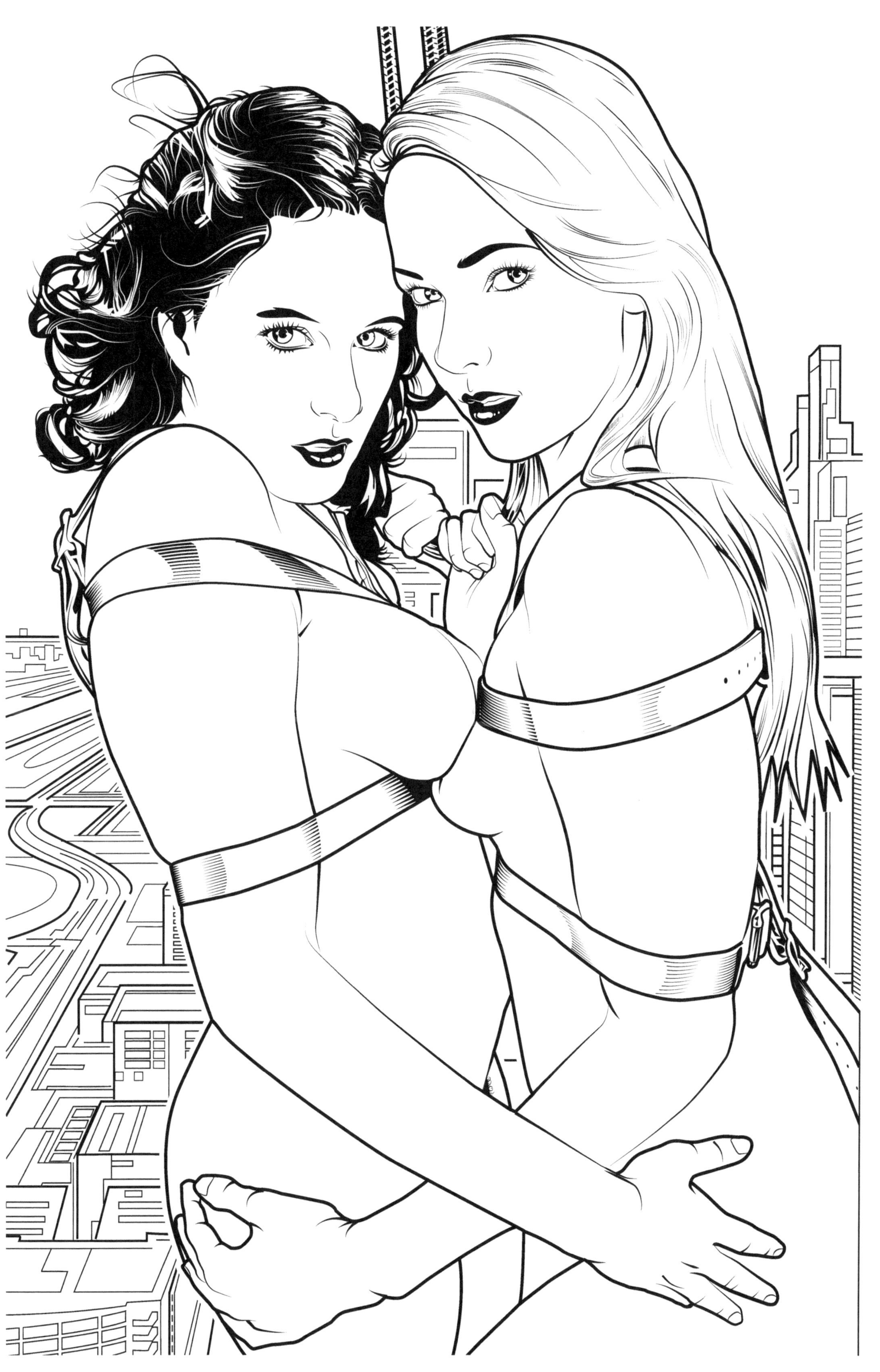

You can count on the creative imaginations of the Mayhems to figure out how to turn nuclear devices into sex toys.

"She's So Hot, She's Radioactive!"

Models: Ned and Maggie Mayhem

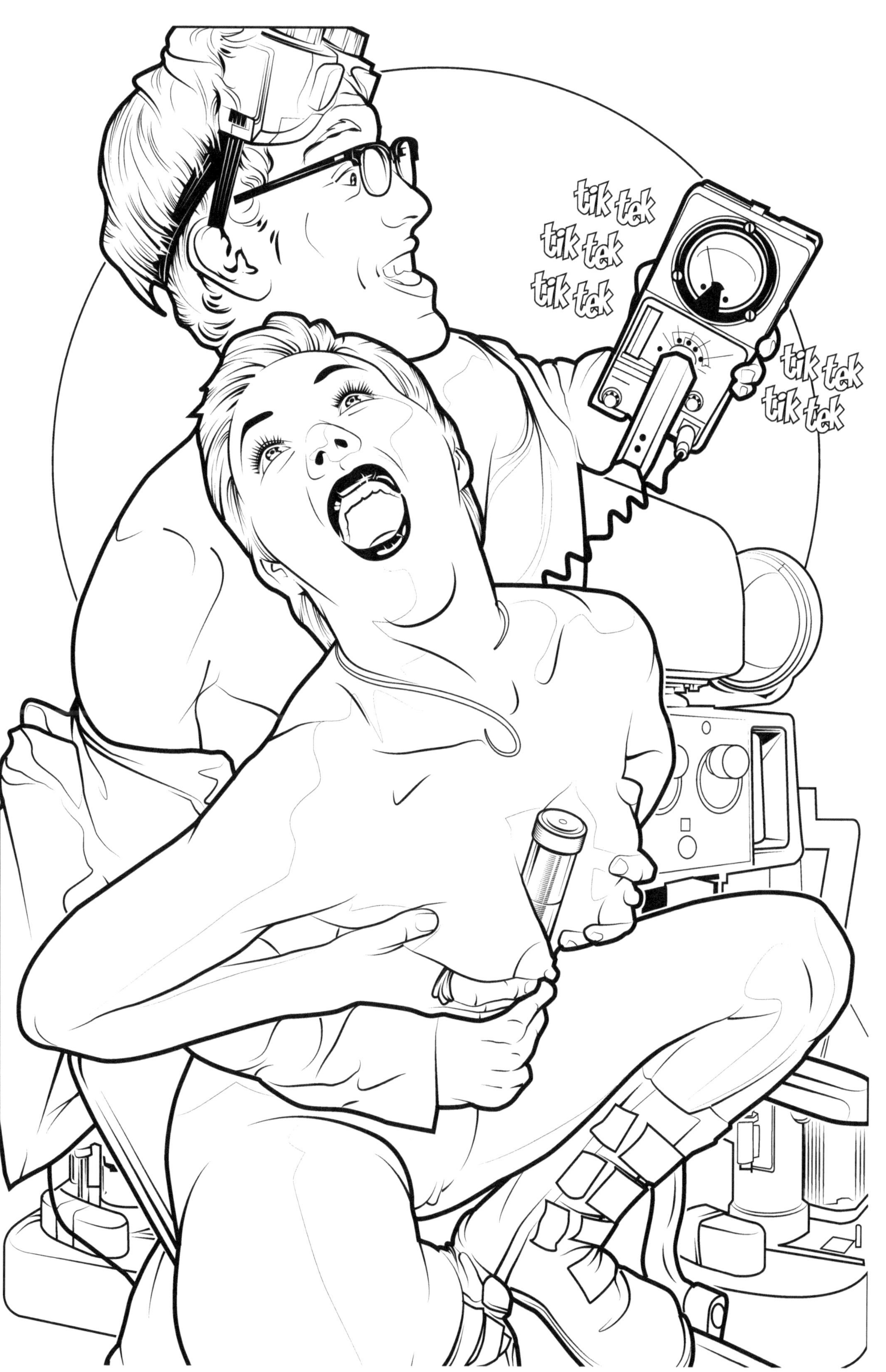
tik tek
tik tek
tik tek
tik tek
tik tek

Now tell us truthfully: who's really afraid of the Big Bad Wolf?

Red Riding Hood

Model: Cat Rich

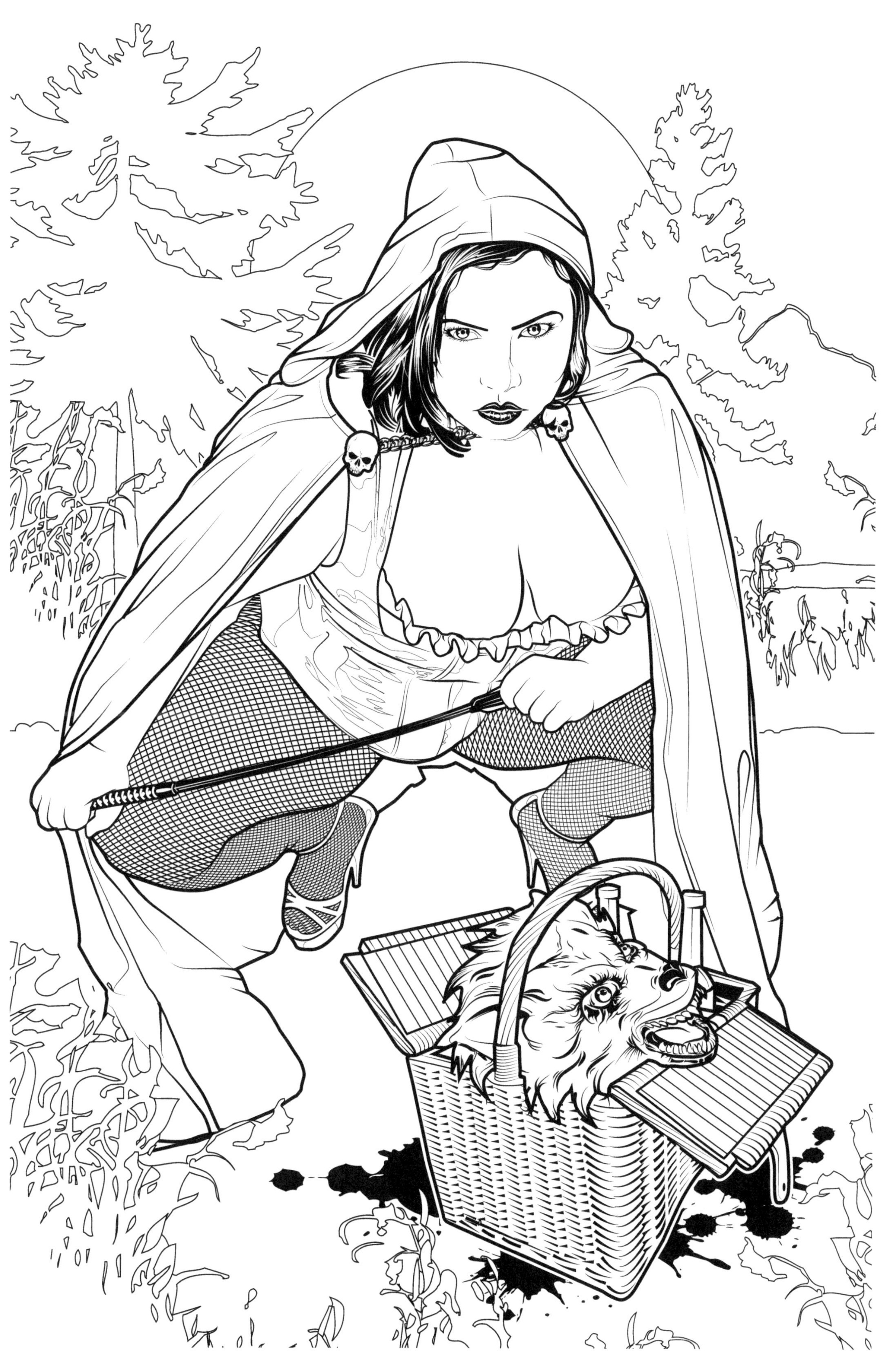

"The path to paradise begins in hell."

Dante Alighieri

Route 666

Model: Scarlet Faux

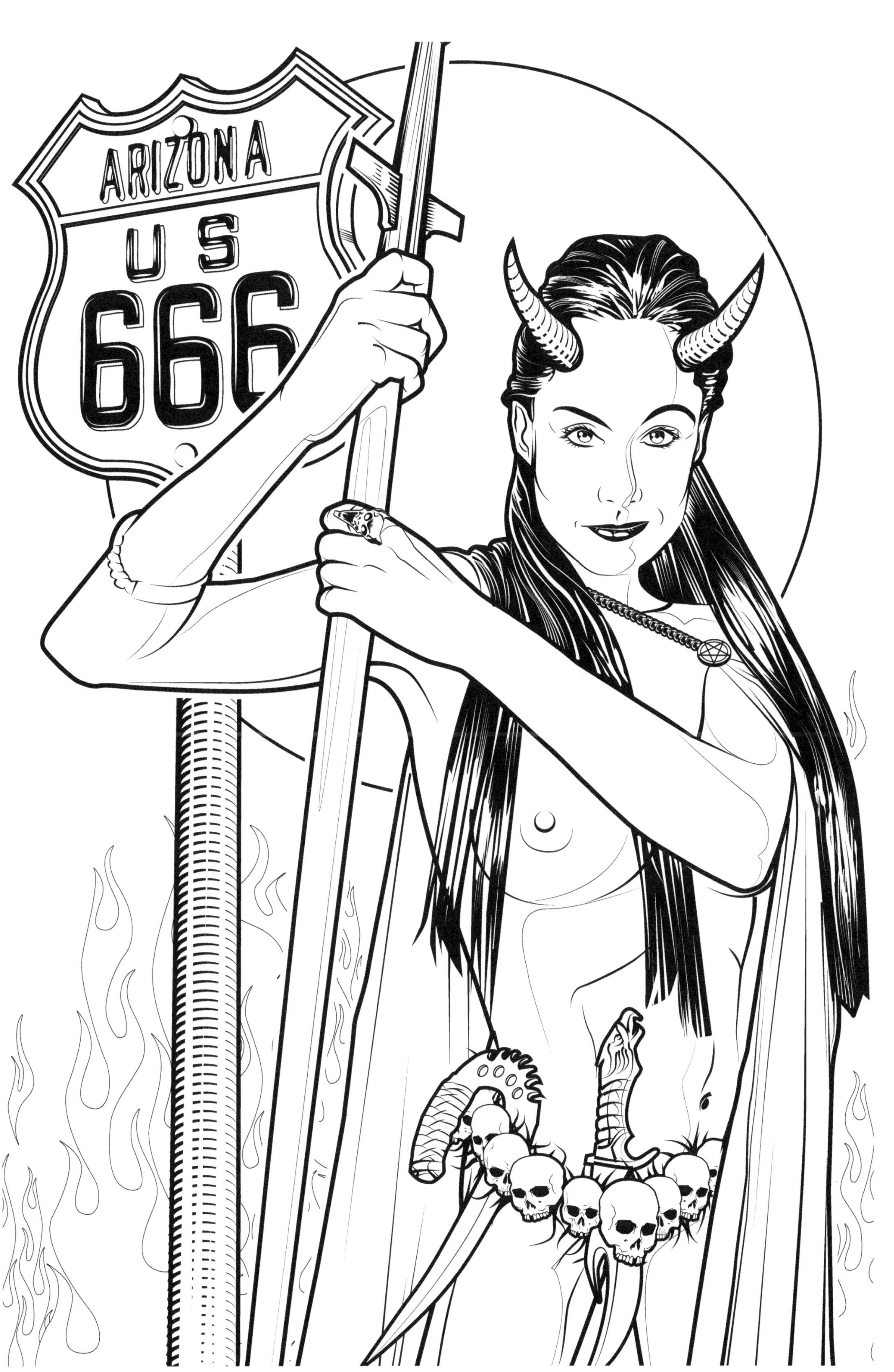
ARIZONA
U S
666

We'd like to thank the people of Cardiff for allowing us to shoot in their city. We promise to keep the body count and property damage down the next time we come into town.

Who's Home

Model: Cherry Katonic

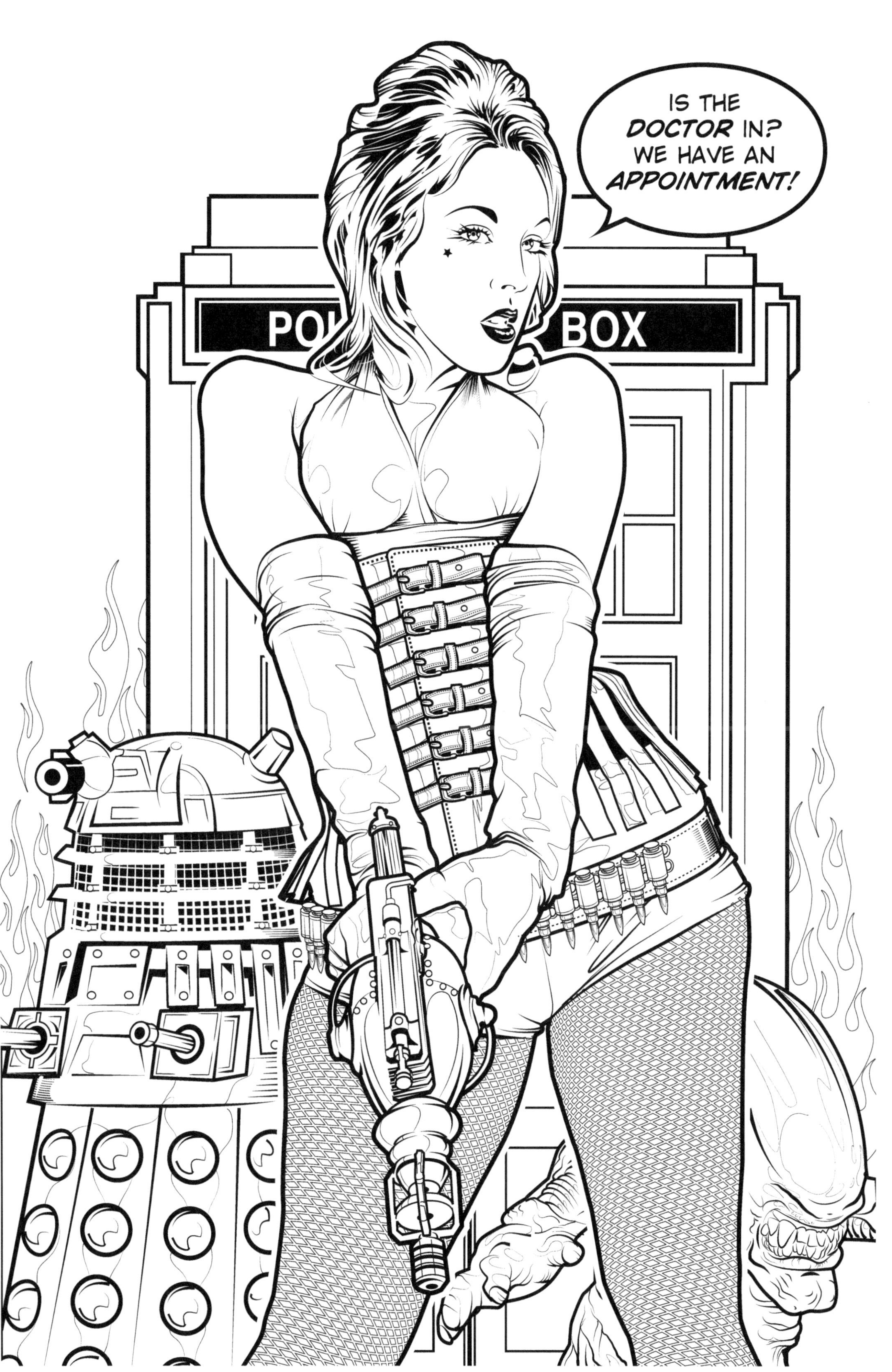
IS THE DOCTOR IN? WE HAVE AN APPOINTMENT!
POLICE BOX

Yeah, Death is like a creepy old pervert at a party. You spend most of your time trying to avoid him and yet he still finds a way to corner you in the end.

Flirting With Death

Model: Dizzy Night

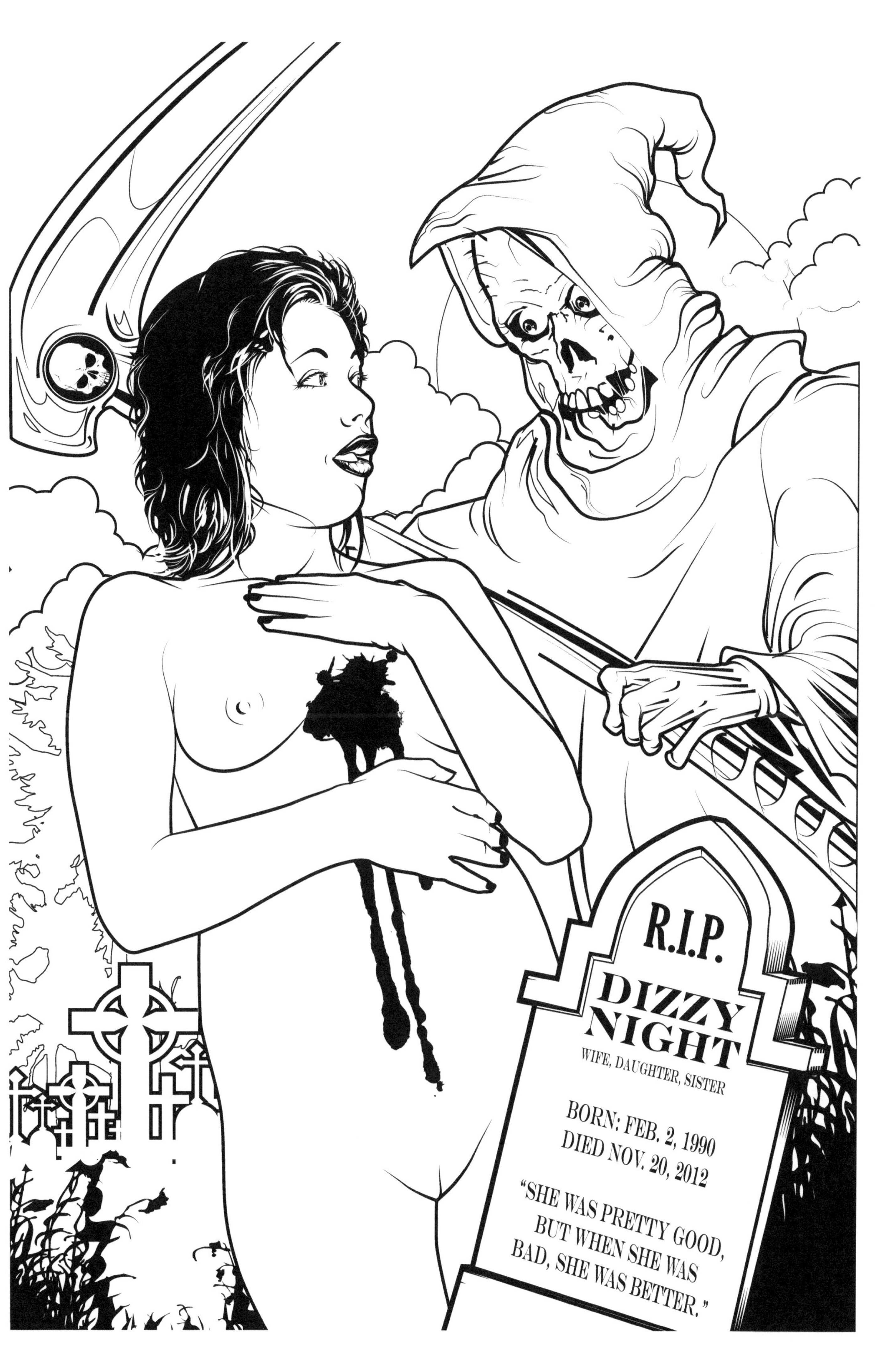
R.I.P.
DIZZY NIGHT
WIFE, DAUGHTER, SISTER
BORN: FEB. 2, 1990
DIED NOV. 20, 2012
"SHE WAS PRETTY GOOD, BUT WHEN SHE WAS BAD, SHE WAS BETTER."

I actually have quite a few friends that work with animals and help do Pet Adoptions for shelters from time to time. Mostly the pets they place are dogs, cats, rabbits etc... Somtimes one of the two legged ones gets taken home, too.

Finding A Loving Pet

Models: Mauv and her boy

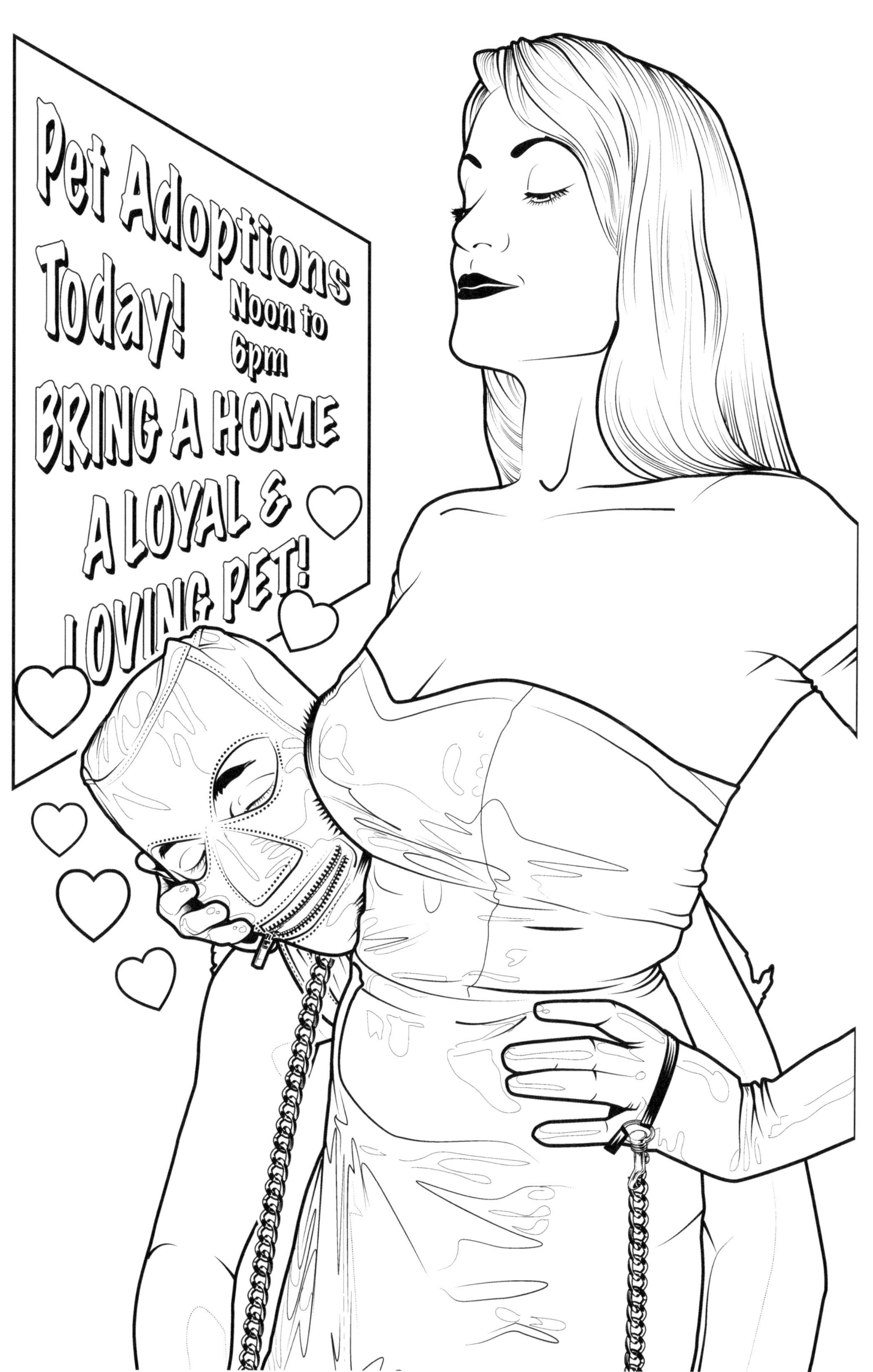
Pet Adoptions Today!
Noon to 6pm
BRING A HOME
A LOYAL &
LOVING PET!

I'm sure if Starfleet Academy ever had a class on how to have sex with alien cultures, Maggie Mayhem would be the instructor. I can see her telling all those young cadets (male, female and genderless species) to always "boldly go where no man has gone before"!

Xenosexuality

Model: Maggie Mayhem

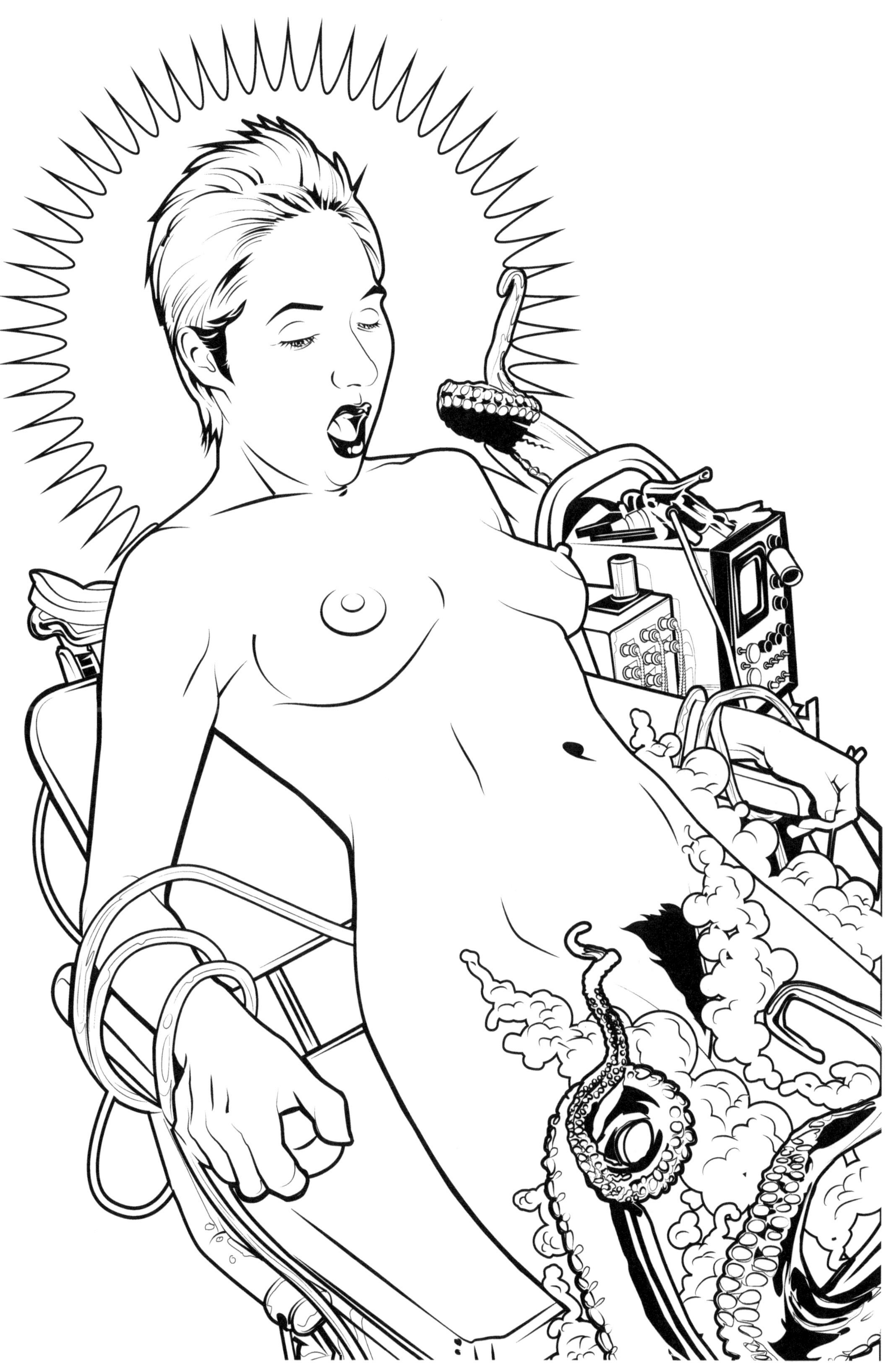

The complaint that I usually have about a lot of erotica out there, is that it can be too dark and serious. The figure tends to be no more than an object to project your fantasies on. On the other hand, I have always liked the moments when you see a flash of an individual's personality. Kink is often described as play, and play is supposed to be fun! So one of the major goals I have always had for my art work is to try and capture that joy and playful spirit.

Happy Sub

Model: HisDame

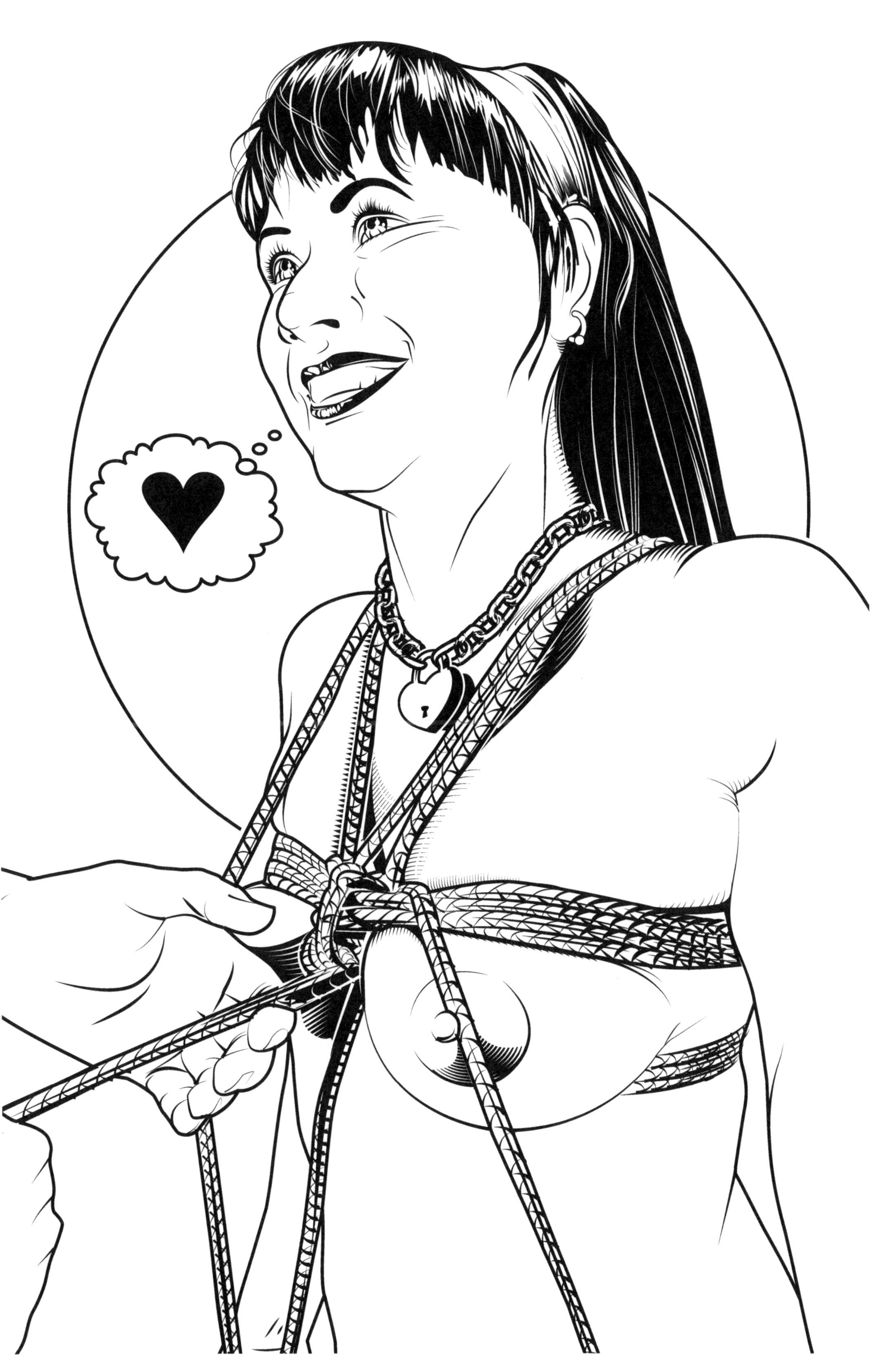

I think the amount of loving tenderness you will find in the sadistic clown scene is greatly overlooked and understated.

Nice And Comfy?

Models: Heart-On and Ringmaster

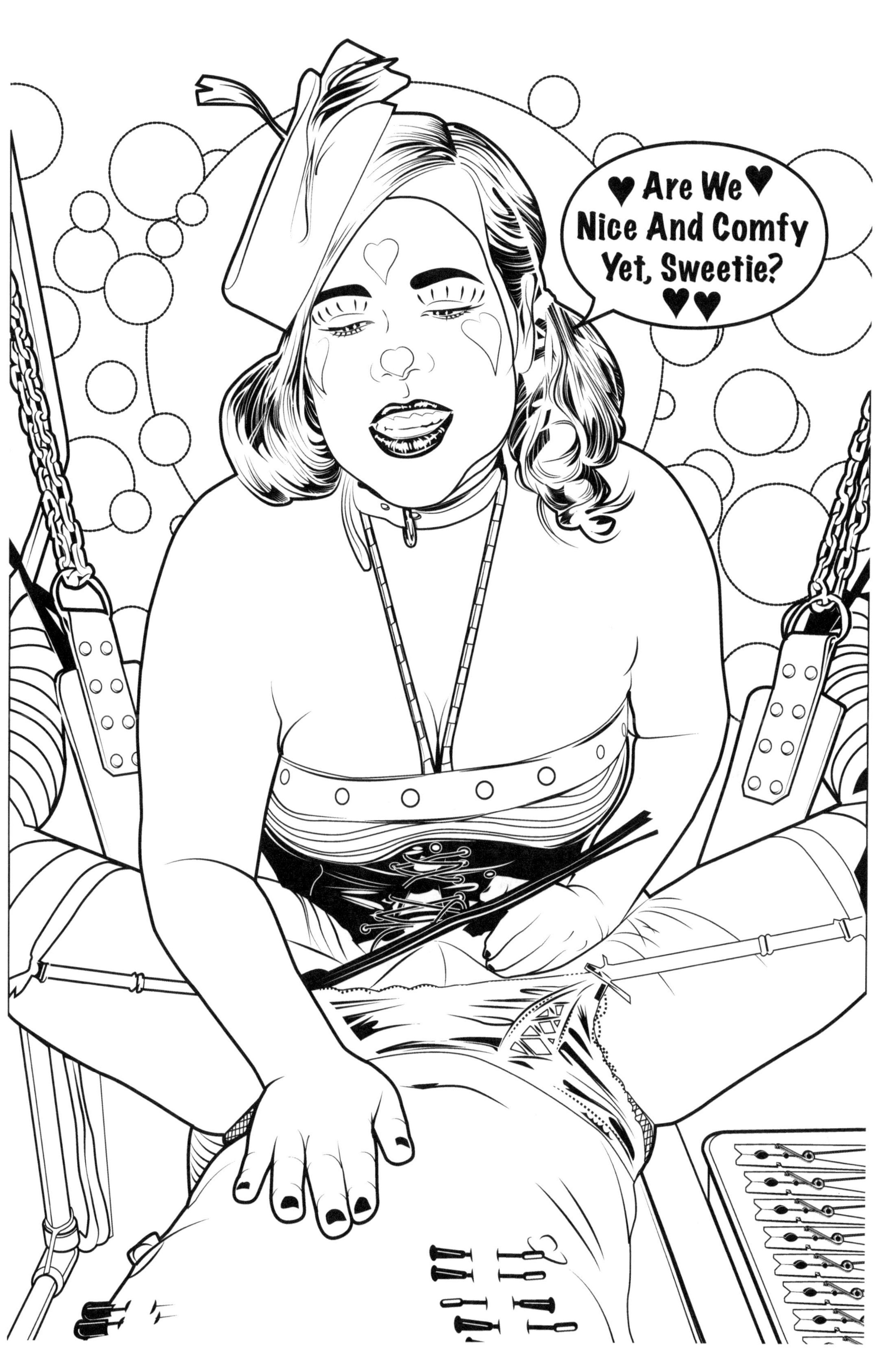
♥ Are We ♥
Nice And Comfy
Yet, Sweetie?
♥♥

Once the first Kinky Coloring Book was published, it seemed the only sane course of action was for me to start work on a second. This was the first image I did for this book. I think Eleanor's expression of fear and anticipation kind of reflected my own feelings at the time I drew it.

Roped Eleanor

Model: Eleanor, Rigger: CorruptMorals

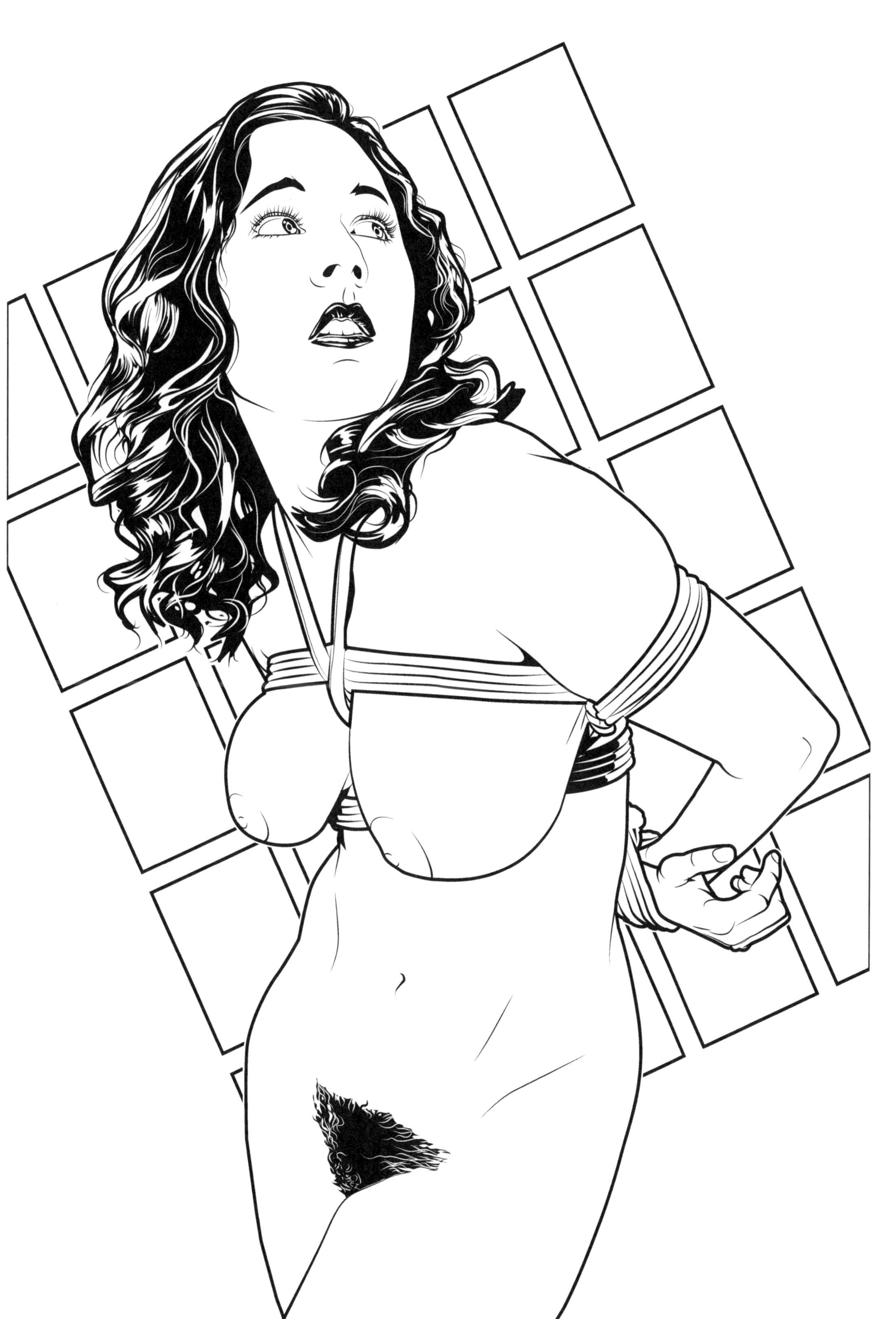

After a life like yours, you didn't really expect to get away with just a warning and reincarnation did you?

Divine Judgement

Model: Mellissa Yvette

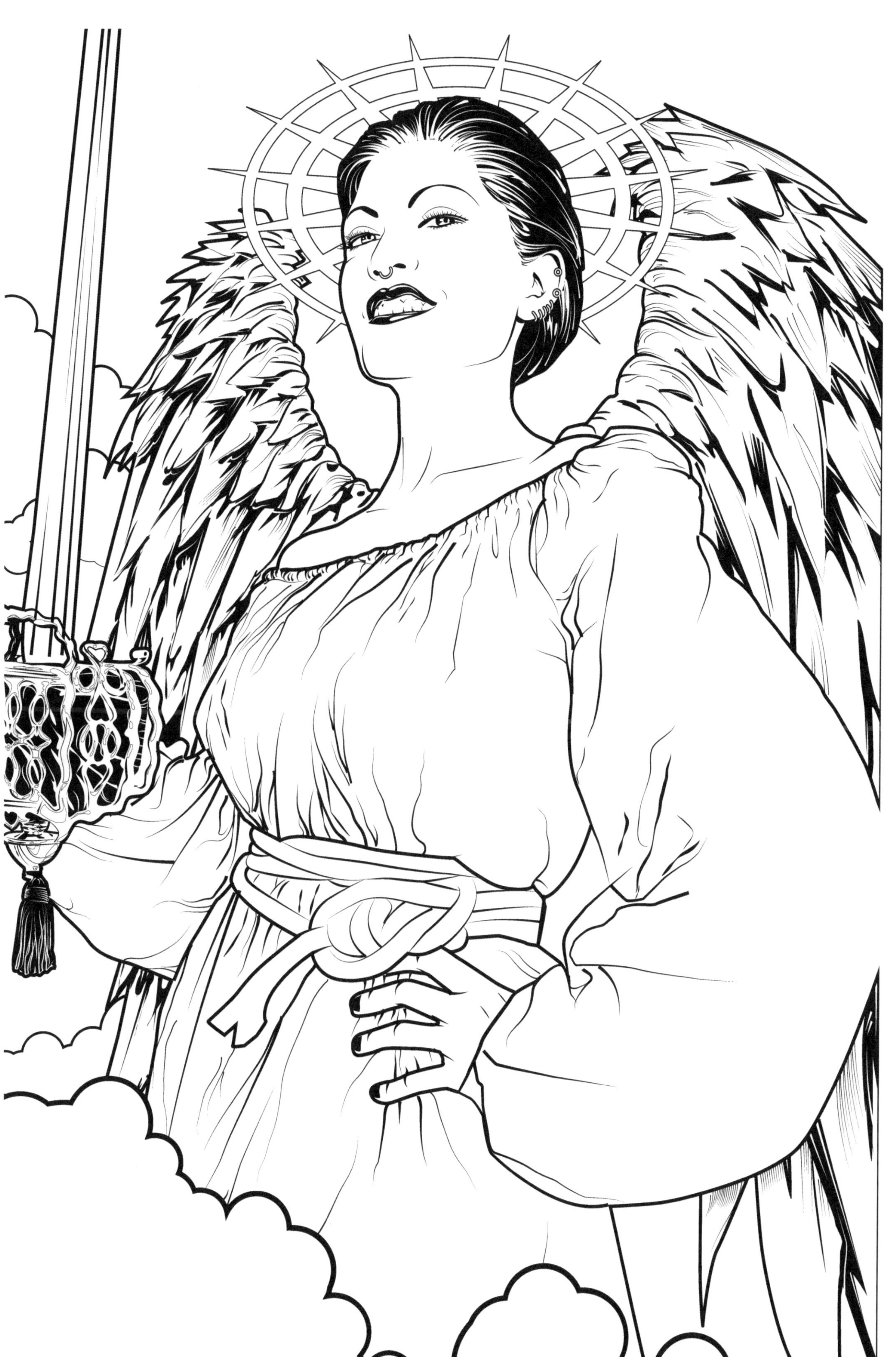

I don't think people appreciate how much patience it takes to be a good fetish model.

The Things I Do For Art!

Models: CorruptMorals, Raven Le Faye, Melissa Yvette
Rigging: CorruptMorals

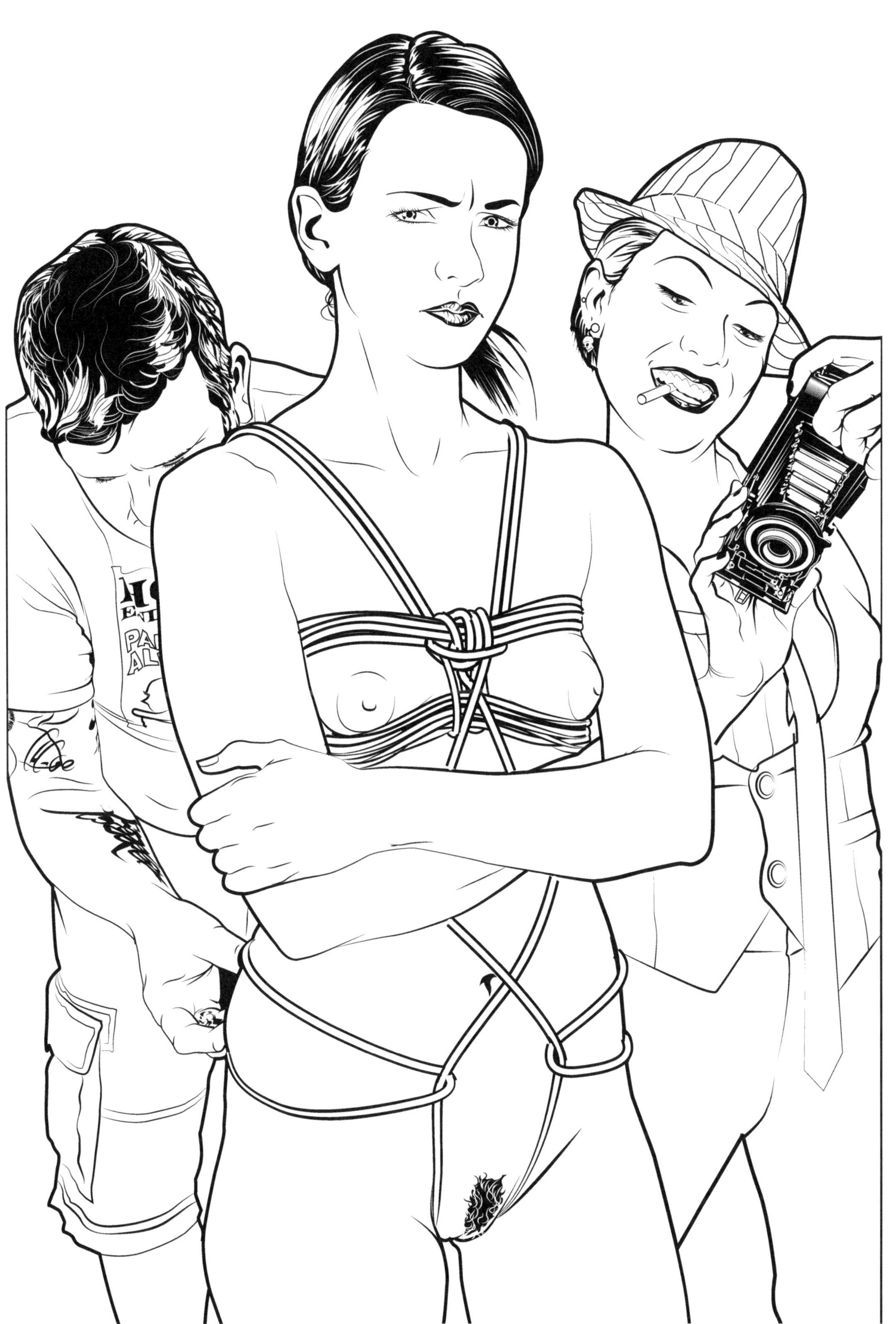

Every Halloween Chelsea bathes in the blood of photographers who have wronged her during the past year. Foolish souls that cancelled at the last minute, didn't send her pictures afterwards or touched her inappropriately.

Blood Bath

Model: Chelsea Christian

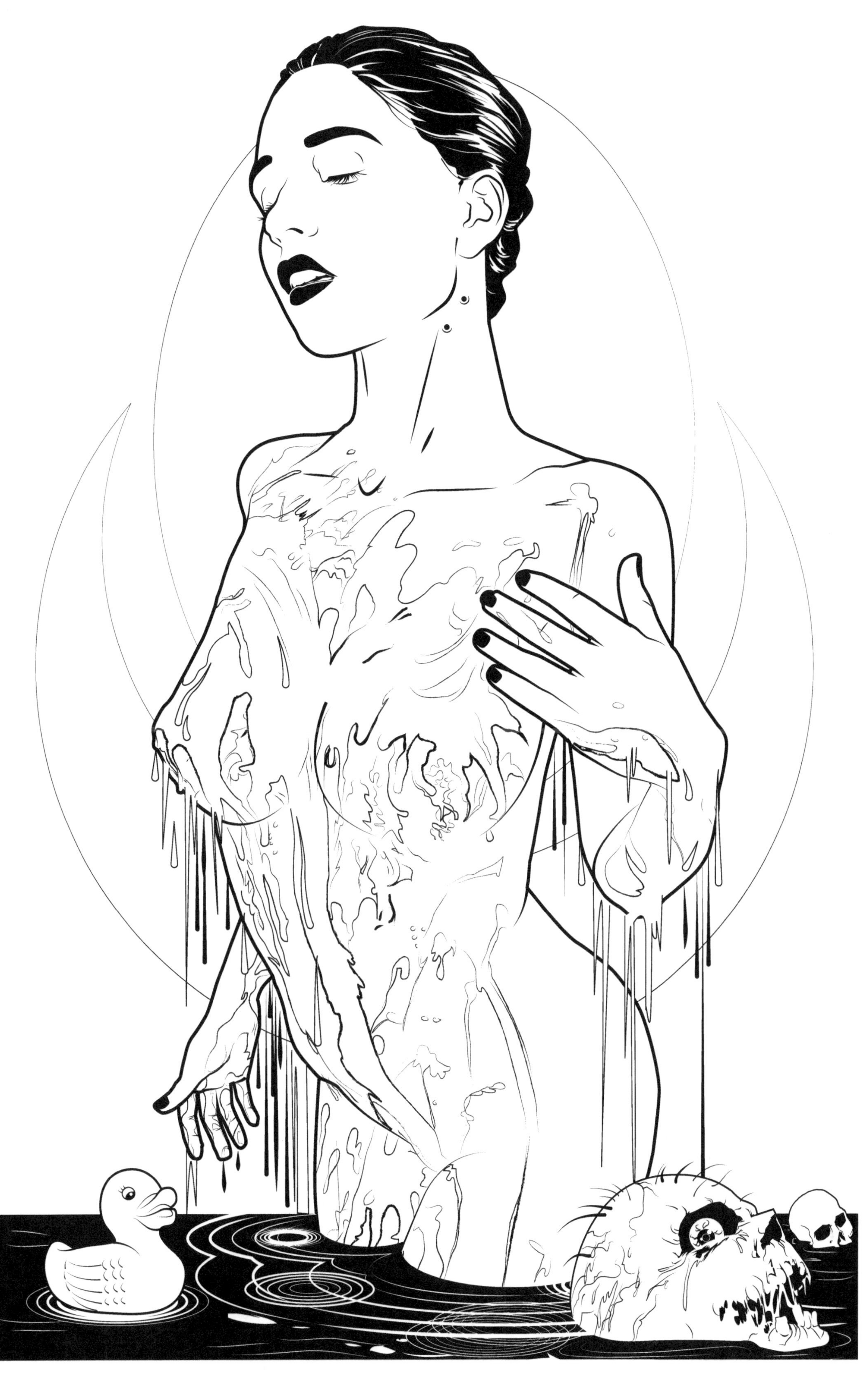

The townsfolk never bothered to question why the Sheriff would always choose to go to a gun fight in just boots and panties. They just knew she never lost one.

Deadshot

Model: Melisande

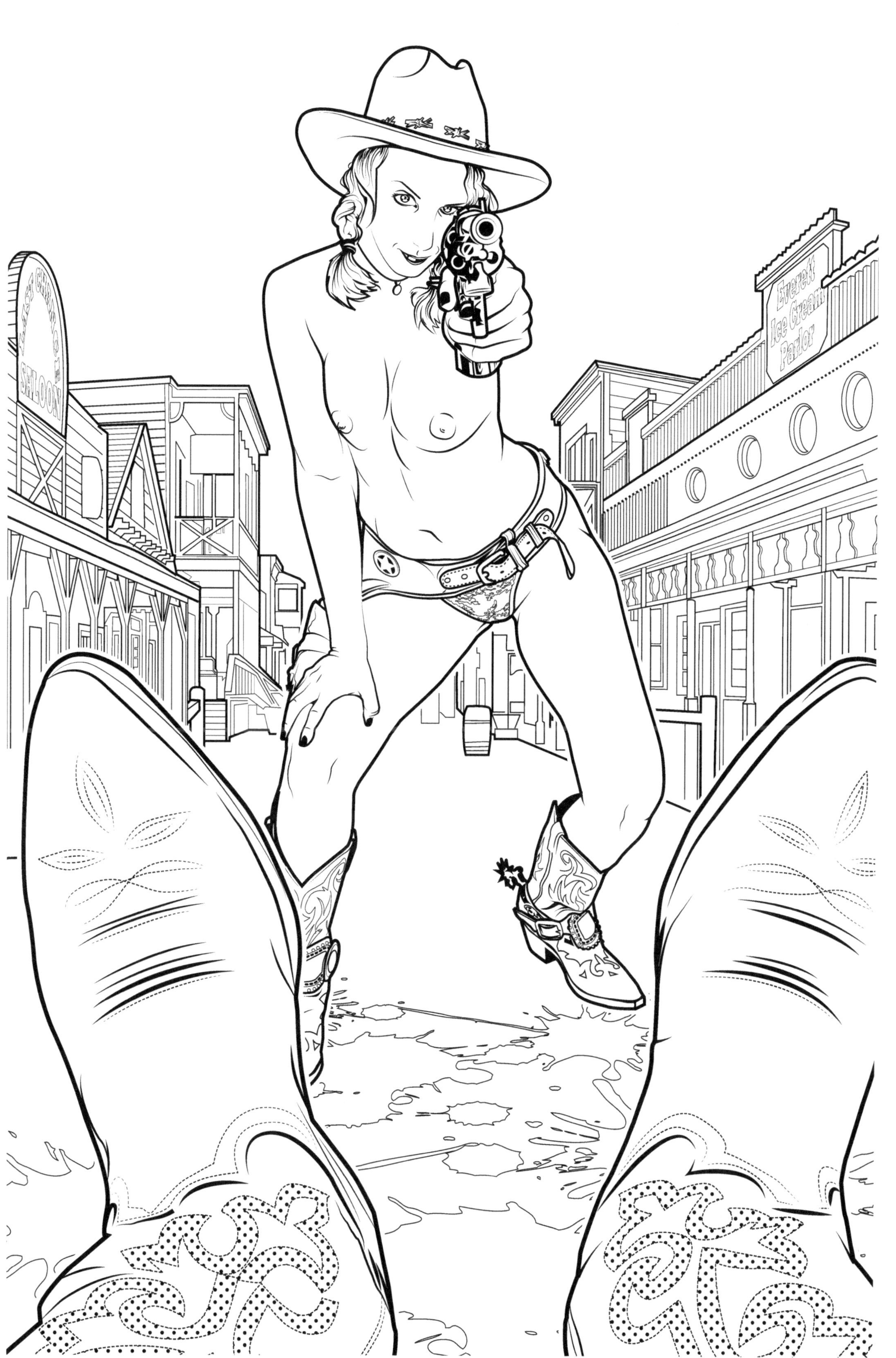
SALOON
Everett
Ice Cream
Parlor

Chelsea giving you the bird.

Spade's Girl

Model: Chelsea Christian, Dress: Lust Designs

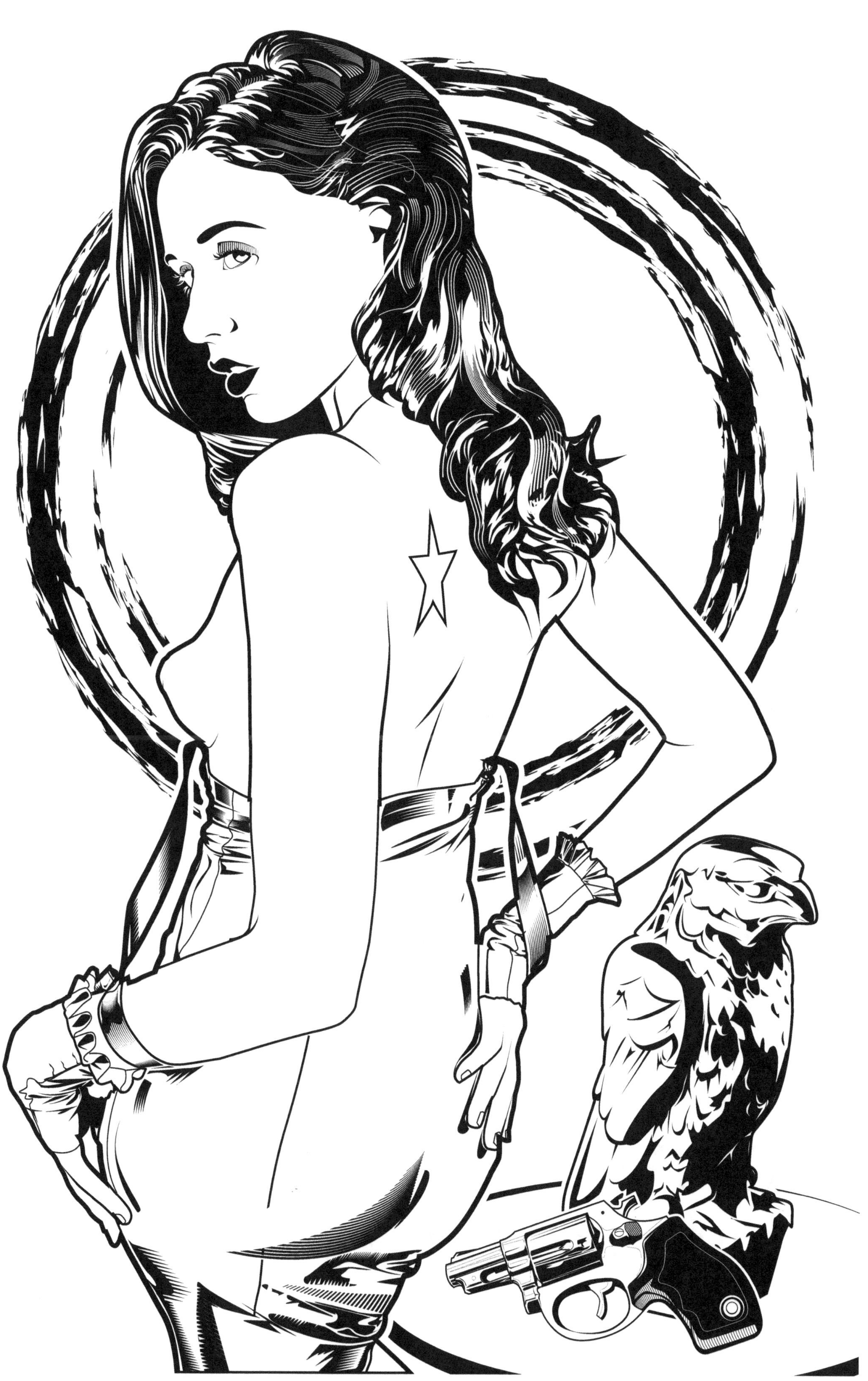

This is the stuff that happens to you when you don't follow Captain's orders!

Mermaid Warning

Models: Dizzy Night & Jeff Cathcart

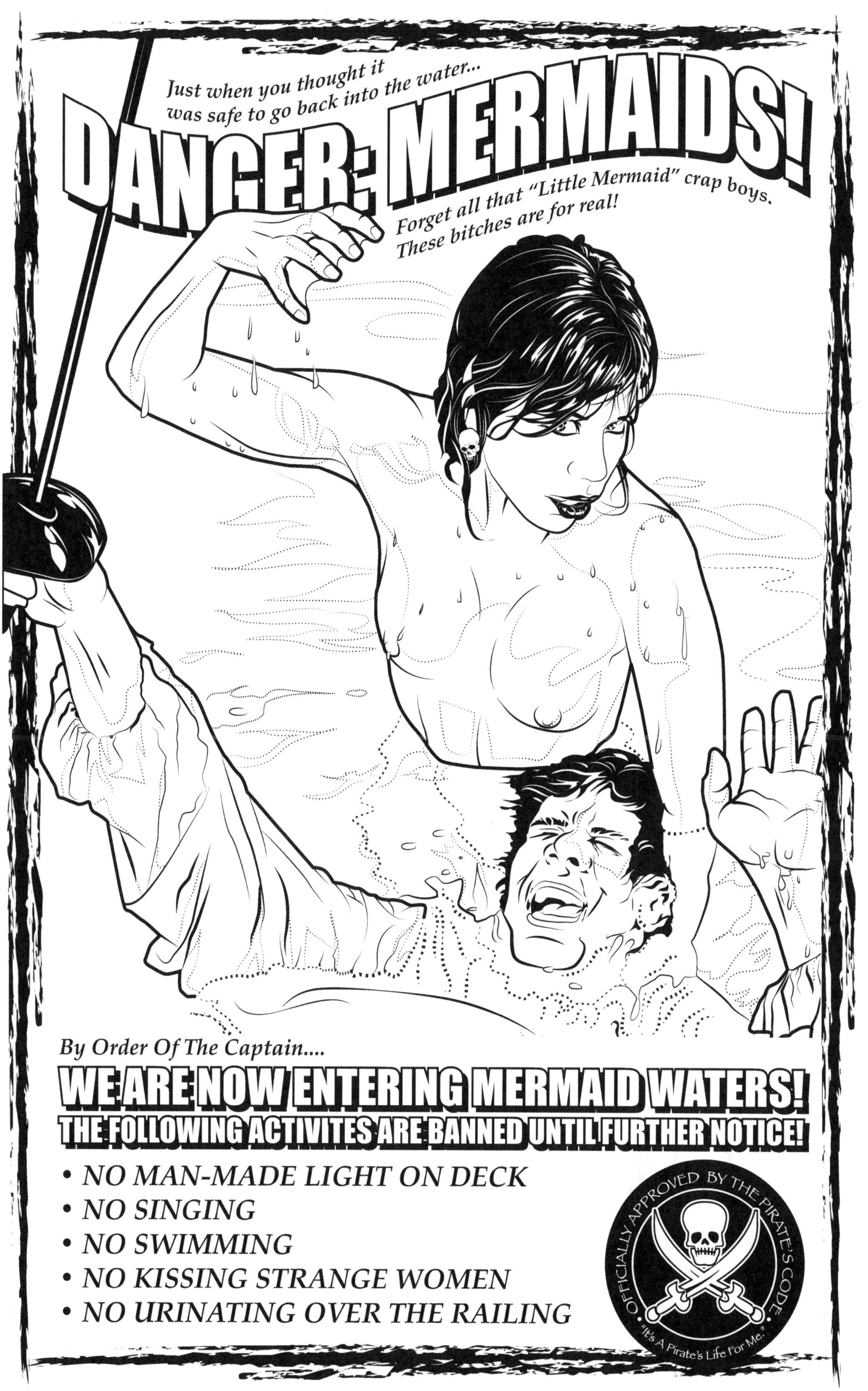

Just when you thought it was safe to go back into the water...

DANGER: MERMAIDS!

Forget all that "Little Mermaid" crap boys. These bitches are for real!

By Order Of The Captain....

WE ARE NOW ENTERING MERMAID WATERS!

THE FOLLOWING ACTIVITES ARE BANNED UNTIL FURTHER NOTICE!

- *NO MAN-MADE LIGHT ON DECK*
- *NO SINGING*
- *NO SWIMMING*
- *NO KISSING STRANGE WOMEN*
- *NO URINATING OVER THE RAILING*

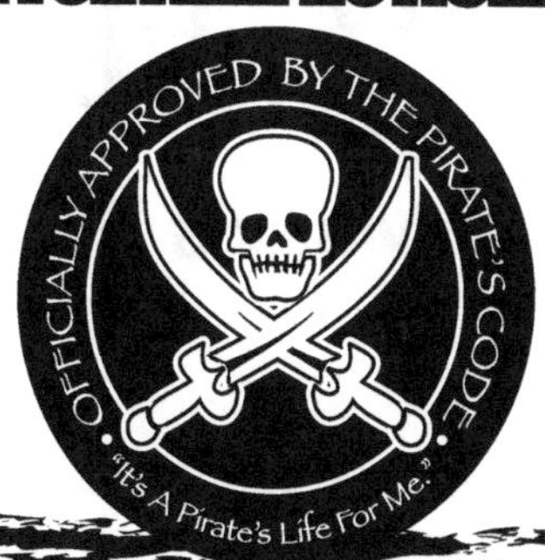

Remember, Toy Story started with a "Woody" too.

Boy Toy

Model: Maev's Boy

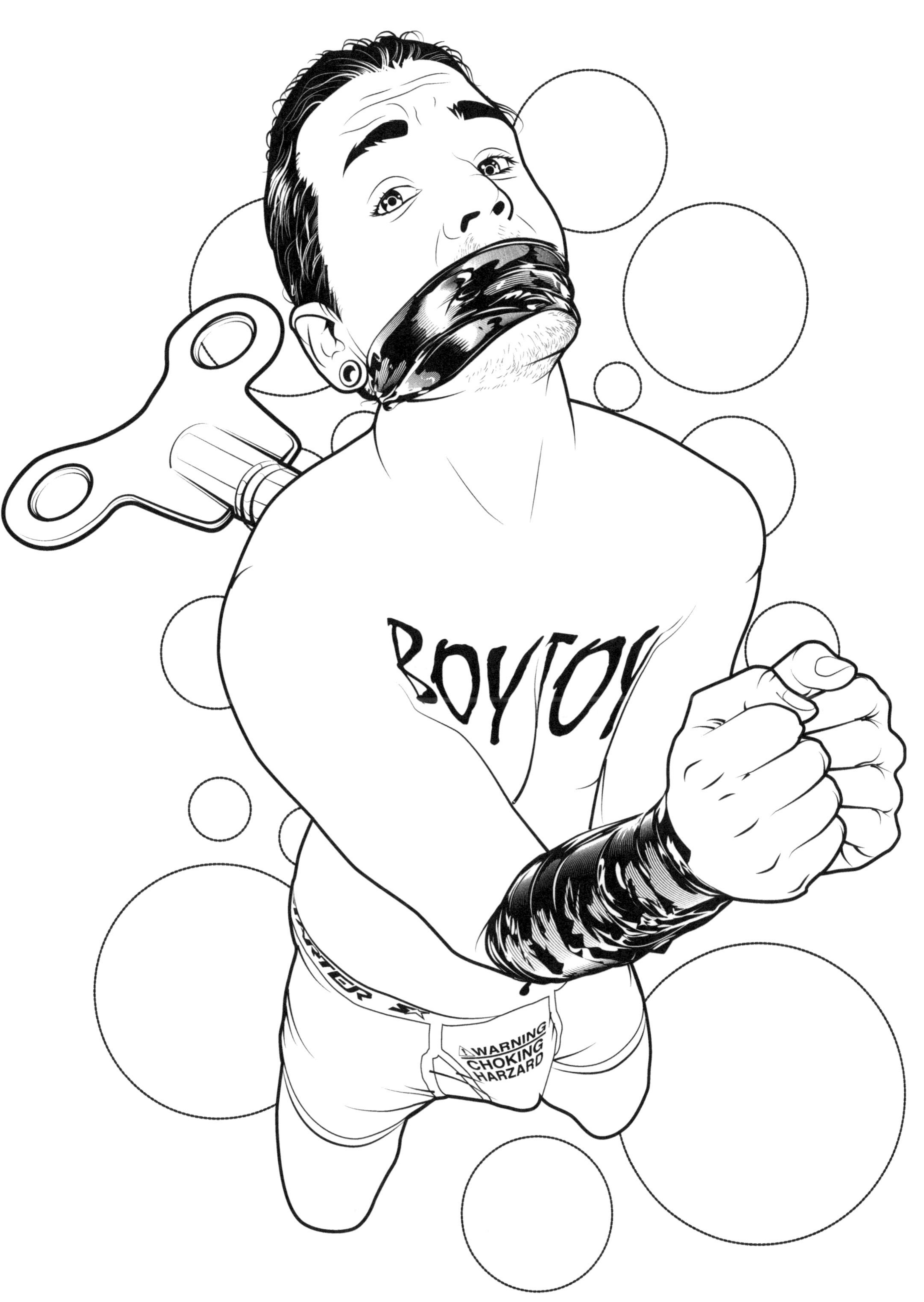
BOYTOY
WARNING
CHOKING
HARZARD

Since this book starts with FreakyMar5's face on the first page; it is only fitting that it ends with her butt on the last one.

The End

Model: FreakyMar5, Chain Rigging: CorruptMorals

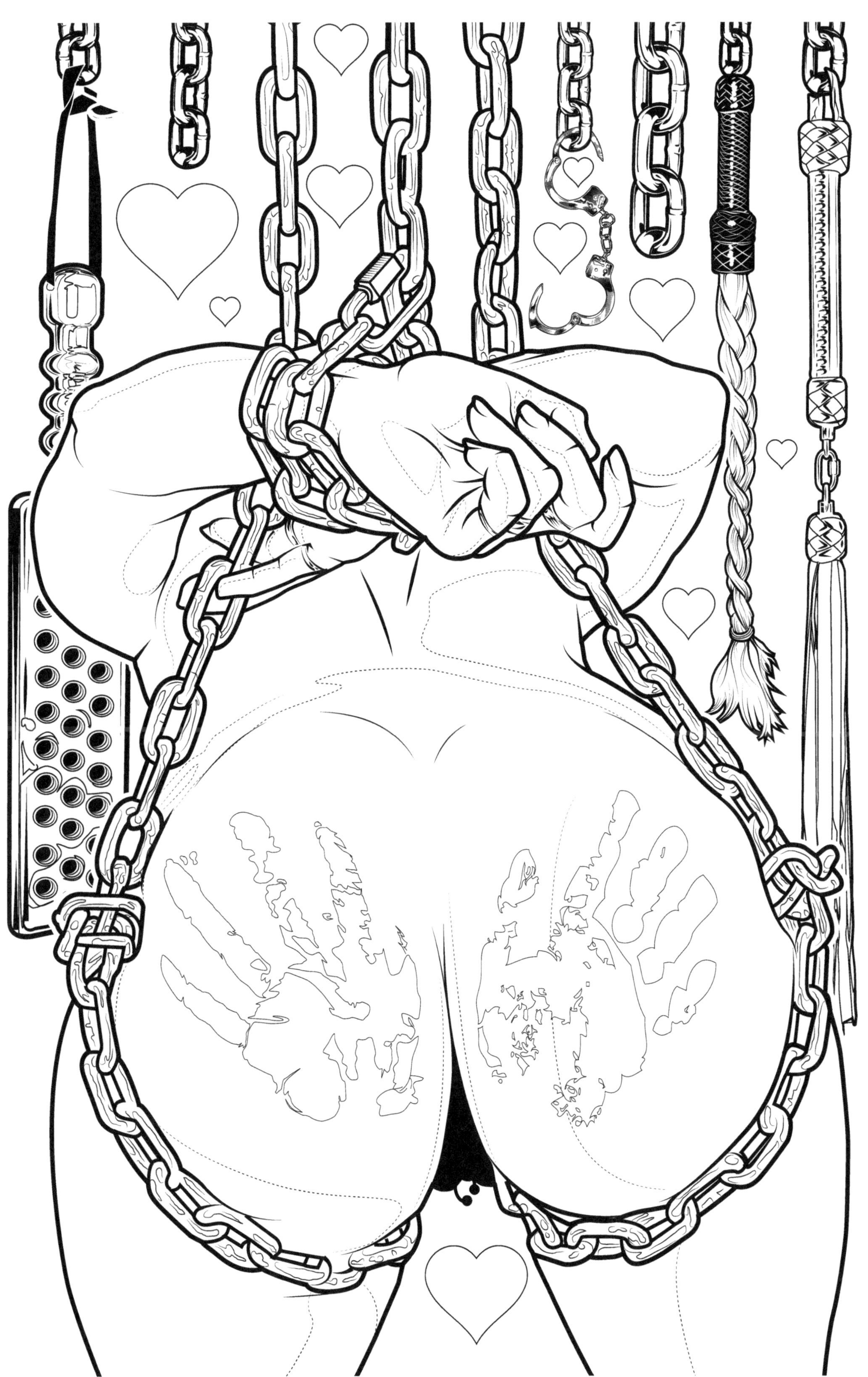

www.ingramcontent.com/pod-product-compliance
Lightning Source LLC
LaVergne TN
LVHW081150110826
845149LV00008B/1616

* 9 7 8 0 9 8 5 8 9 9 9 1 2 *